MISSING PERSONS
book one

The Rose Queen

m. e. rabb

speak
An Imprint of Penguin Group (USA) Inc.

The Rose Queen

SPEAK
Published by Penguin Group
Penguin Group (USA) Inc.,
345 Hudson Street, New York, New York 10014, U.S.A.
Penguin Books Ltd, 80 Strand, London WC2R 0RL, England
Penguin Books Australia Ltd, 250 Camberwell Road, Camberwell, Victoria 3124, Australia
Penguin Books Canada Ltd, 10 Alcorn Avenue, Toronto, Ontario, Canada M4V 3B2
Penguin Books (N.Z.) Ltd, 182-190 Wairau Road, Auckland 10, New Zealand

Published by Speak,
an imprint of Penguin Group (USA) Inc., 2004

3 5 7 9 10 8 6 4

Produced by 17th Street Productions,
an Alloy company
151 West 26th Street
New York, NY 10001

17th Street Productions and associated logos
are trademarks and/or registered trademarks of Alloy, Inc.

SPEAK ISBN 0-14-250041-0

Printed in the United States of America

For my sister Jackie, with love

REWARD: $5,000.00 USD
SOPHIA SHATTENBERG

MISSING—SUNNYSIDE, QUEENS—NEW YORK, NEW YORK, USA

NAME: Sophia Shattenberg
RACE: Caucasian
AGE: 15
DOB: February 12, 1988
HAIR: Brown, wavy, long
EYES: Brown
HEIGHT: 5'2"
WEIGHT: 100 pounds
DISTINGUISHING FEATURES
- Rub-on tattoo of the Froot Loops toucan on her left wrist. May have rubbed off.
- Mole on right cheek.

LAST KNOWN LOCATION: 39–89 48th St., Sunnyside, NY
SUSPECTED LOCATION: New York City, NY
AGENCY NAME: Queens County Police Department
PHONE NUMBER: (718) 345-6549
CONTACT NAME: Enid Gutmyre (relation: stepmother)
PHONE NUMBER: (212) 555-3432

Sophia "Sophie" Shattenberg was last seen at her residence, 39–89 48th St., Sunnyside, New York, on July 9, 2003, at 2 A.M. She was wearing a pink T-shirt, men's boxer shorts (blue polka dot), and fuzzy slippers in the shape of sharks. If you have any information at all regarding the whereabouts of Sophia Shattenberg, please contact the Queens County Police Department or Enid Gutmyre. You can also e-mail the Missing Persons Index at info@misspers.net.

REWARD: $5,000.00 USD
SAMANTHA SHATTENBERG

MISSING—SUNNYSIDE, QUEENS—NEW YORK, NEW YORK, USA

NAME: Samantha Shattenberg
RACE: Caucasian
AGE: 17
DOB: April 2, 1986
HAIR: Brown, curly, short
EYES: Brown
HEIGHT: 5'4"
WEIGHT: 130 pounds
DISTINGUISHING FEATURES

- Appendectomy scar
- Extremely curly hair

LAST KNOWN LOCATION: Dime Savings Bank, 46–10 Queens Boulevard, Sunnyside, NY
SUSPECTED LOCATION: New York City, NY
AGENCY NAME: Queens County Police Department
PHONE NUMBER: (718) 345-6549
CONTACT NAME: Enid Gutmyre (relation: stepmother)
PHONE NUMBER: (212) 555-3432

Samantha "Sam" Shattenberg was last seen at the Dime Savings Bank ATM at 46–10 Queens Boulevard, Sunnyside, New York, on July 8, 2003, at 10 P.M. She was wearing a T-shirt emblazoned with "Bronx Science Math Team," blue jeans, and white Nike tennis shoes. If you have any information at all regarding the whereabouts of Samantha Shattenberg, please contact the Queens County Police Department or Enid Gutmyre. You can also e-mail the Missing Persons Index at info@misspers.net.

One

Three days after our father died, my sister woke me up in the middle of the night and told me to start packing.

I squinted at her. "Are you sleepwalking again?" She'd gone through a sleepwalking phase a couple of years ago when she was fifteen, bursting into my room and yelling ridiculous, incomprehensible things like, "The tissues are coming!" and "Stop the elves!"

"Hurry up. We don't have a lot of time," she said, ignoring my question. She had brought one of our parents' old black suitcases into my room; she pulled open my dresser drawers, then began to throw piles of my underwear, winter sweaters, and flannel pajamas into the open suitcase.

I gaped at her. "What are you *doing?*"

"We have to go," she said. "We have to get out of here."

I pulled off the covers and put on my shark slippers. My first thought was that we were going on some kind of vacation. It wasn't a bad idea—we both needed to get away. Being in the house by ourselves was unbearable. The brick house in Queens, which we'd lived in our whole lives, seemed to echo and rattle with the fact that both our parents were gone now. Our mom had died six years before, and you would think that after that much time you'd get used to it, but I hadn't. Everything in the house made me miss my mom—her navy-blue pea coat hanging in my closet, her photos on my shelf, her silver locket in my jewelry box. And now my stomach clenched every time I glanced at my father's wool cap dangling from a hook in the hall, the piles of mail addressed to him that still arrived relentlessly, and the grocery list in his familiar handwriting taped to the fridge, alongside his medication chart.

I still kept expecting him to shuffle down the hall in his sheepskin slippers, asking me, "You're not getting on the subway in a skirt that short, I hope?"

"Yeah, I am," I'd say. My skirts were never *that* short.

"Sopheleh," he'd say, and shake his head.

I should've prepared myself for the possibility of him dying. He'd struggled with heart disease ever since our mom died; he was on so many medications that he had to make checklists to remember to take them. His doctors had said that he had a high chance of having a heart attack, but the risk never seemed real. Then, three days ago, he just didn't come down for breakfast in the morning. We thought he was sleeping late, but when Sam went up to wake him, she screamed my name, and as soon as she did, I felt dizzy and numb. Which was how I'd felt ever since.

Sam stared at the suitcase on my floor, looking like she was about to hyperventilate. I finally just started throwing things in it to appease her. All we'd done for the past three days was mope around in a comalike state. Earlier that day, after the funeral, we'd sat shiva, the Jewish ritual to mourn a death. I couldn't believe that just that morning, we'd watched our father's body being lowered into the grave beside our mother's. It had been raining, and my sister and I had huddled beneath a Snoopy umbrella. *You will always be with us,* our mom's headstone read. Was that true? I'd cried so much in the past three days that I couldn't even wear my contact lenses; my eyes were too swollen. I had to wear the monstrous thick plastic-rimmed purple glasses that I hadn't worn since sixth grade. The rabbi droned on in Hebrew— *"El Maleh Rachamim . . ."*—and I looked at my sister and thought, *We have nobody now. It's just us.*

And there we were, just us, in my bedroom with a half-packed suitcase on the floor between us. Sam sat back on her heels and said, "I've figured out how we can run away."

"What are you talking about?"

"Leaving. For real."

"You're crazy," I said. "Where are we gonna go? We can't just leave. We're still sitting shiva. And I—I'm baby-sitting tomorrow. And we don't have any money—"

"We have money. I have it all planned out. And we can't wait any longer—we have to go *now.*"

She was shoving more and more of my stuff into the suitcase, as much as she could fit.

"If we don't leave now," she said, "when Enid inherits everything, she's going to ship you off to that boarding school in God knows where, and God knows how long will it be until we see each other again. The most important thing, no matter what, is that we stay together. That's what I promised Daddy—that we'd stay together. Enid made the same promise to him, but we know she's not going to keep it."

We'd joked about running away ever since our dad had married Enid—a tall, wiry woman who called us "the young ladies" in the same tone she used for "the rodents in the subway." Enid spent most nights in her apartment in Manhattan, which she'd kept during her whole two-year marriage to my dad. Whenever she did make it out to our house, she found things wrong with everything we did— the dishes weren't clean enough; the house was too dusty and cluttered; I played my music too loud and my clothes were too tight; Sam studied too much, her haircut made her look like a boy, and she needed to lose weight.

Then there was the time, about six months before, when I'd overheard Enid talking on the phone to her mother.

"The Langmoor Academy," Enid had said in her gravelly voice as she took notes. "Sounds perfect for the younger one."

That was how she referred to me—"the younger one."

"What's the Langmoor Academy?" I'd asked her later that night, when we were alone together in the kitchen.

"It's a fine boarding school in Alberta, Canada," she'd said. "I've been trying to come up with a plan for your future, in case . . ." She lowered her eyes. "With the exchange rate, tuition's practically free." She went on to say that the school focused on rehabilitating unruly youths by packing them off on outdoor adventure trips, like climbing the glaciers of the Yukon. No joke. The school probably charged only a little bit extra to permanently lose one of their pupils in an abandoned ice cave or to toss them into a flaming volcano.

I'd told my father what Enid had said. He'd simply responded, "I know Enid would never do that. There must have been some kind of misunderstanding. She'd do her best by you. She loves you very much." He trusted her. To her credit, he'd been happier since he married her than he'd been in a long time. Still, I wished my dad could have seen through her. Enid had brought up the Langmoor plan again that afternoon, at the funeral reception. "They have room for you this fall," she'd told me. So she really was serious about sending me away. Children, to Enid, were something to be endured, like the flu, until they could be passed on to someone else.

I'd thought that the talk about running away had been just a joke—though apparently Sam had been taking the idea a little more seriously than I had.

She stared at my Scooby-Doo alarm clock. "We have thirty minutes to get out of here."

"What about NYU?" I asked Sam. Even though she was only seventeen, she had graduated from high school a couple of weeks ago and was supposed to start college in less than two months.

"I'm postponing it."

"Why? You've been planning on it—"

"I've been planning on *this*," she said. "I'll go to college—we'll both go to college. But it's important that we can both *afford* to go to college and not be so far away from each other. That's why we need to get out of here."

"How much money do you have? Five dollars? A hundred? We don't have enough to live on. I have, like, ten dollars." I waved at the tiny purple piggy bank on my dresser, covered with scratch 'n' sniff stickers.

Sam took a deep breath and looked down at the suitcase. "Actually, we have about three hundred thousand."

My throat dried up. "What?"

"We have three hundred thousand dollars." She seemed kind of surprised, and pleased, to hear the amount stated so plainly out loud.

"You're kidding."

She shook her head. "I figured out a way to transfer Daddy's money into our names. Well—our new names. Felix helped me. That's why—that's where we're going now, to his place, to trade in the car and get some new IDs for ourselves."

Felix was one of Sam's best friends from school; he operated a fake-ID business out of his basement. Sam closed the suitcase and zipped it up, then started dragging it down the stairs to the door.

I couldn't believe this was happening. "You stole Daddy's money?" I asked as she opened the kitchen door.

"Could you keep it down a little?" She made sure no one was eavesdropping outside, then shut the door again. "It's not stealing. That money's rightfully ours—it's Mommy's life insurance and Daddy's life savings. If we stay, everything goes to Enid—everything. She wouldn't let Daddy leave the money in a trust, with her as the fiduciary, no: it was all to her or nothing. So the money's all hers now. Or it's supposed to be."

I blinked at her. "What are you babbling about? Judiciaries?"

"Fiduciary. Help me with this suitcase. It means Enid would be in control of the money, but she'd have to spend it for our benefit. But that's not how it will be now. Now she can blow it all on Weight Watchers Fudgsicles or weight-loss programs for her mother, and there'll be nothing we can do about it."

Enid meticulously recorded every penny she spent, and recorded every calorie she ingested on her PalmPilot. Once she made my dad drive around to four different stores, looking for her twenty-calorie Fudgsicles.

We loaded the suitcase into the car, but I still wasn't convinced that we were actually going to leave. Back in the kitchen I told Sam, "I just think—there must be something we can do. You'll be eighteen in a few months—can't you be my legal guardian or whatever? I can stay with you. Or I can get court permission to be on my own—I saw that on *Law & Order*." These had been my secret plans whenever I let my mind wander about what would actually happen if our father died, which had only been a few times. I always thought that if I imagined it, then I might somehow make it happen. And he had seemed fine before he died—I knew he had his heart problems, but he looked the same as always. I think a part of me believed he'd live forever. Or at least a long, long time.

"There's no guarantee that I'd be allowed to be your legal guardian or that you'd get that court permission," Sam said.

"Then we can contest the will—"

"You think a judge would really decide against Enid

and a legal will in favor of two teenagers?" She shook her head. "No way. And there's the most important thing—we can't be separated. No matter what, we're staying together, and no one can stop us from doing that."

I stared at her. I couldn't even imagine what it would be like if we were apart. And she was right—it didn't matter to Enid. If anything, it seemed she would almost take pleasure in seeing us split up. She'd never liked the bond that Sam and I had.

"Listen, Sophie, we can't stay here all night arguing. Just pack up your stuff and we can talk about it more in the car."

Maybe we didn't have any other choice. I started putting my things into shopping bags. A part of me didn't mind the idea of leaving—the house felt like an empty box without our father in it. Abandoned and deserted. We couldn't keep living there, pretending that things hadn't changed. They *had* changed, and we had to do something, and I had no idea what we should do. At least Sam had a plan.

And maybe we were only going away for a little while. "We're coming back sometime, right?" I asked Sam.

She hesitated. "Yeah. Sometime."

I hoped she was telling the truth.

I loaded my things into more suitcases and shopping bags. "We have to fit it all in the car," Sam said, "so only take what you really need."

I needed everything. I packed my mom's pea coat and my dad's wool cap. I packed all my jewelry and makeup, and my two hair dryers (regular and travel), and all my hair gels and body powders, my straightening iron and my hot rollers. I scooped everything hanging in my closet into a Hefty bag.

I kept going back into the house for more stuff—all my photo albums, the scrapbook I'd made of our mother, and my Martin guitar. My father's cotton T-shirts and his sweaters, which still held his warm, comforting smell, like spices and soap. My magazines. A bunch of my favorite books, though I couldn't bring them all. I made sure to take *The Complete Sherlock Holmes*—my dad's old hardcover copy that he used to read to Sam and me—and a full set of *Anne of Green Gables*, which my mom had bought me. I also threw in some other favorites—*To Kill a Mockingbird*, *The Little Prince*. I knew there would most likely be bookstores and libraries wherever we were going, but I wanted my copies of these books with the pages I'd folded over and read and loved—the pages my parents had touched.

Sam had packed earlier—the car was already loaded with her suitcase, laptop computer, printer, and file folders.

She shook her head as I kept making trips back and forth to our dad's Toyota. It looked like it was about to split open from all my stuff. "Sophie, there will be stores wherever we end up. You don't need to bring everything you own. Someone's going to see us."

"No one's going to see us," I said. The houses on our block were dark. Occasionally someone walked by down the sidewalk, but nobody we knew. "And this is the last of it."

"All right," she said. "Are we ready?"

"Wait." I ran back inside for Ed, my stuffed polar bear—I'd left him on my bed. I also grabbed my Scooby-Doo clock, my nail polishes, and my father's beloved framed Brooklyn Bridge poster from the living-room wall.

"Nothing else is going to fit in here," Sam said. She leaned against the car, with her arms folded.

"Okay," I said. "This is it. I've got everything." Though even as I said it, my heart sank at the idea of everything we were leaving behind. Furniture I loved and plants, paintings, our parents' flower-patterned sheets, and a million other things I would miss. I'd lived in that house my whole life. I just couldn't get used to the fact that it was only Sam and me now. It made me feel like a different person, that we had no parents anymore. In movies I'd seen and books I'd read, it had always seemed like orphans were these strong, indomitable people who could overcome and conquer anything—but I just felt so *not* strong, so *not* capable at all.

Sam shoved Ed into a crevice in the trunk and slammed it shut. I stared around our neighborhood. The old attached brick houses and tiny yards. The alley-way behind our house where we used to play hide-and-go-seek and kick ball. The fact that we were leaving, that this might be the last time I ever stood here outside our house in our neighborhood, didn't sink in. Nothing felt real—not the sound of Sam turning on the ignition or of me closing the door, or the sight of our house disappearing as we turned the corner.

Two

A chill swept through me as we drove down the Long Island Expressway. I'd never done anything illegal before—unless you counted the time my best friend, Viv, and I shoplifted lipstick at Rite Aid and got caught three minutes later by the security guard.

Sam's friend Felix lived in Bayside, Queens, a twenty-minute drive from our neighborhood. He was one of the smartest kids at her school, though he didn't always use his brains for legal activities. He supplied a huge portion of New York City high school students with their fake IDs. He was rich from it. Sam had become friends with him in her forensic biology class—her high school, Bronx Science, offered what seemed like a hundred different science electives. They learned how to dust for finger-prints and how DNA testing was done, all that kind of stuff. Though I think Felix took the class not because he was interested in catching criminals someday, but because he was interested in not getting caught himself.

Now I wondered if that was why Sam had taken the class, too—as part of her grand scheme.

"Why didn't you tell me you were planning this?" I asked her. "I mean, how long have you been putting this whole thing together?"

She shrugged. "I don't know. Maybe a year and a half. I guess I started thinking about it around six months after Dad married Enid."

"Why didn't you tell me? Did you think I would blow it or something?" My voice rose.

"Calm down. I just thought it would be easier to pull off if I kept it a secret. I thought about telling you a hundred times. Believe me. But it would've made it too hard to get things ready. And then you'd have it hanging over your head, too, you'd be worrying—and you'd also be at fault if we got caught. Anyway, you know now."

"This is my life, too. And I'm not a total idiot. I can keep a secret."

I often had the feeling that Sam never took my opinions that seriously because I was younger than she was and a voice student at La Guardia School of the Arts instead of a mathematician and scientist like she was. And I wasn't so careful with money or even that interested in it, like Sam was—she was always reading the stock pages of *The New York Times* and *Money* magazine and watching *Wall Street Week* on PBS. I think poking a stick in my eye would be more fun than watching *Wall Street Week*. But I still thought she should have trusted me. "I mean, we have math classes at my school, too," I said. "We don't just sit around singing do-re-mi all day."

"I know," she said. "I just thought it was safer to do it this way."

I stared down at my feet. I was still wearing my slippers; in the rush I hadn't even bothered to change. I took them off and fished a pair of sandals out of the mess in the backseat. I reached into one of the Hefty bags and pulled out a black miniskirt and put that on, too.

"Oh no," I moaned.

"What?" She jerked the steering wheel and the car swerved.

"I left my tube top in the dryer—my brand-new tube top."

"We're not going back for your tube top," she said sternly.

My voice caught. "I know," I said quietly.

Felix Marino lived on a pretty, tree-lined street with old-fashioned streetlamps on the corners. He made enough money from his fake-ID business to support his mother and sisters in the Philippines. He lived with his aunt, who worked as a night nurse; she was gone all night and slept all day.

Felix hugged Sam as she walked in the door and then hugged me. He wore glasses as thick as Coke bottles, bright green flip-flops, and a blue bathrobe.

"So you're doing it," he said to Sam.

"We are." She smiled.

"I told Difriggio to expect you," he said.

"Who?" I asked.

"Tony Difriggio—he's my friend in Indianapolis."

"But who is he?"

"He's my . . . mentor, so to speak. He put me in business."

"Mentor? I didn't know petty criminals had mentors," I said. "Is it like Big Brothers Big Sisters or something?"

Felix ignored my sarcasm. "Difriggio's a great guy. He's going to help you out when you get to Indy."

I stared at Sam, my body going cold. "Indy? Is that where we're going—*Indianapolis?*"

She gave Felix a look.

"Um, let me give you the grand tour," he said to me, clearing his throat. "Since you've never been here before."

He was obviously proud of the operation he'd set up, and as we descended two steep flights of stairs into an abnormally deep basement, he rattled off the names of the different machines he kept down there—optical scanners, encoding machines, embossers, laminators, and more. I stopped listening to his descriptions because all I could think about was that we were going to Indiana. Why Indiana, of all places? There was only one reason I could think of, and it made me shiver.

"Why can't we go to the Bahamas or Bermuda?" I asked Sam. "Or Malibu? Or Bali? Somewhere warm, with guys on the beach in those little tiny swimsuit things, and sun, and—"

"We need to be somewhere where we have a contact, someone who can get us even more paperwork completed, and someone who can help us keep an eye on the police so that we don't get caught," she said.

"You can't do better than Difriggio," Felix said. "He practically runs the state of Indiana. The underworld side of it, that is. He can help you out in a dozen ways, ways I don't even know about."

I slumped against a whirring white machine. "This is so crazy."

"He's a nice guy," Felix said. "His grandma sends him homemade ravioli from Brooklyn every week."

"Oh, great," I said. "Ravioli."

"All right, we have to do the pictures," Felix said. "For the license and the passport."

"Pictures?" My hair was in knots from running around crazily, packing the car, and my eyes seemed almost permanently red from crying so much during the past few days.

"Did you get the dye?" Felix asked Sam.

"I have it." Sam took off her blue backpack and reached inside. "Here, this will cheer you up," she said to me. She pulled out a Rite Aid bag, which held two boxes of Clairol Hydrience Absolute Blondes hair dye.

I picked up the boxes. "Ooh. Ivory Moon and Oasis. Can I do Ivory Moon?" I'd always wanted to go blond.

After we made a mess in Felix's bathroom, Sam and I emerged as two blondes. I also used some cover-up to hide the mole on my right cheek—a last-minute brainstorm of Sam's. I thought we looked much better than we did as brunettes. Sam couldn't have cared less about how she looked.

Felix made me stand against a white board. I took off my glasses, and he snapped a photo. He took Sam's picture, too, then disappeared behind a few machines. A little while later he reappeared with a manila envelope.

"Here they are. License, insurance, and registration for Sam and passport for Sophie."

I stared at my first passport. *"Fiona Scott?"* I read aloud.

"I had to change one of your names, because it's not safe to have two sisters listed on the books anywhere as Samantha and Sophia. Sam's official name is now 'Sam' instead of Samantha. And people you meet can still call you Sophie—just tell them it's your nickname. Anyway, I thought Fiona was kind of close to Sophie."

"Fiona? Close? Are you kidding me?" How was I going to start my new life as *Fiona?*

"It's a great name," Felix said, seeming personally insulted that I wasn't happy with it.

"Hmmph," I grumbled. "Fiona Scott. Is this Ellis Island or something? We're not Jewish anymore?"

"The whole idea is to blend in," Sam said. "Think of it as a stage name."

I stared at the passport. I looked like a squinting, bushy-haired maniac. A blond one. From Ohio.

"I gave Sam an Ohio license—Ohios are much easier to produce than New Yorks," Felix explained, glancing proudly at his work.

Next Felix gave us a cell phone with preloaded hours and no traceable account number, then led us upstairs. I stared at my wrist as I held the banister, looking at the Froot Loops tattoo that Viv had put on me at the funeral reception to cheer me up. She'd joked that Froot Loops tattoos were part of the Korean

way to sit shiva. "I need to call Viv before we go," I
told Sam.

Vivien Chun had been my best friend since the first
day of seventh grade, when we'd sat next to each
other in Ms. Weissman's earth science class. We'd
played hangman through the whole class and after
school gone shopping on Greenpoint Avenue. We
bought sweet rice and bean cakes at the Korean grocery store and ate them while we watched *General
Hospital* at her place. I'd talked to her nearly every
night on the phone for the last three years. I had to
call her now.

"You can't," Sam said. "Nobody can know what
we're doing."

"But—"

"She's right," Felix said. "It's too dangerous."

"But *you* know," I said to Felix.

"That's different," Sam said. "Felix is helping us."

"Maybe Viv could help us, too."

"Sophie. It's important that we don't tell anyone, or
else we really might get caught."

I couldn't believe this. As if losing our dad wasn't
enough, I had to lose my best friend, too? I couldn't even
imagine not speaking to Viv again. "But can I e-mail
her?" I asked. "When we stop somewhere?"

"Maybe," Sam said. "Don't worry. You'll see her again."

I hoped she was telling the truth.

Felix poured coffee for us into two *Shakespeare in
the Park* mugs and brought us into his backyard. The
yard was surrounded by a tall fence and hedges so no

one could look in. In front of the garage, parked on the gravel driveway, sat a huge old brown Buick.

"This is it," Felix said, and patted the car. "Your new baby."

It was the size of a boat and dented and scratched; wires hung out of the dashboard. It looked about two hundred years old.

We stared at the brown thing. "What do we do, stick our feet out the bottom and run like the Flintstones?" I asked.

"Ha ha," Felix said. "It was the best I could do. We had to redo the VIN so it's not traceable. Do you know what a pain that is? The VIN's in seven places. It's not easy to cough up an untraceable legal car."

"Vin what?" I asked.

"Vehicle identification number. Every car has one."

Sam sat in it, Felix handed her the keys, and she turned on the ignition. It growled like a bear, then went dead.

"You've got to juice the engine a little," Felix said. "Press down on the gas." He leaned over Sam to look at the dashboard; his bathrobe caught on the car's rusty edge. He tore it loose, leaving several blue threads dangling from the car.

After three tries it finally started and hummed away noisily. Sam brought our dad's car around back, and Felix helped us transfer all our things into the Buick. By the time we finished, it was beginning to get light out. Sam took out the map and laid it on the hood. Felix helped her trace the route. "The Holland Tunnel to 78," he said. "Then 81 to 76 to 70. That's the best way."

"Let's hope this thing makes it," Sam said.

Felix grinned. "It'll make it."

Sam hugged the map to her chest. "Thanks for everything. I owe you big time, you know."

He shook his head. "You don't."

"And—you won't say anything about this to anyone, right? You had no idea we were leaving."

"What do you take me for? An amateur?" He hugged her. "I haven't seen you since eighth-period gym in June."

"Take care of our dad's car, okay? I like that car," I said.

He opened the driver's-side door and Sam climbed in. "I'll find it a happy home, under a brand-new identity, just like you."

"And you'll keep an eye on what's going on with a certain skinny woman who eats three calories a day?" Sam asked.

"I will."

"All right." Sam smiled. "We'll be seeing you." She shut the door.

"I'll be seeing you."

I hovered in place by the car door for a minute, standing in Felix's little driveway. I didn't want to get into that rusty brown car. I wanted to get back into our old car, our dad's car, and go back home, and see our dad sitting at the kitchen table, *The New York Times* spread before him, wearing his gray sweatpants and the Mangy Mutt T-shirt my mom had bought him on Fire Island ten years ago. He'd be eating a bagel and lox and clipping a recipe for low-fat kugel out of the Living section. He'd glance up at us and say, "Look at my girls. How can any man be so lucky, to have two girls like these?"

Sam started the car. "Sophie, are you ready?"

Ready? I would never be ready. Everything had happened so quickly—I didn't know if I'd ever catch up. But I knew I had no choice but to go ahead with this. It didn't matter if I was ready or not.

I got in the car, hoping Sam wouldn't notice I was crying behind my glasses.

I tried to pull myself together as we drove toward Manhattan. Everything was okay, I told myself. Things could have been worse. I could have been freezing to death in an ice cave in the Yukon, wearing only my Langmoor uniform. Instead I was driving to Indiana with my sister.

I hadn't wanted to get too embroiled in the subject in front of Felix, but I wondered if Sam had chosen Indiana because of our mother.

I had the scrapbook of my mom with me in the front seat—it was the one thing I wanted to make sure made the trip safely. In it I'd pasted photos of her, and letters, postcards, and birthday cards she'd written to me, even her doodles on notepads. And several newspaper articles about her.

**Lorna Shattenberg Declared Dead
After Missing for Two Years**

Lorna Shattenberg, the manager of the Clausen Gallery on West Broadway in Manhattan, was declared dead on Tuesday. Mrs. Shattenberg had been missing since June 28, 1997, when she mysteriously disappeared while on a business trip to Indianapolis, Indiana. Donald Burgee of Evanston, Illinois, was charged with Mrs. Shattenberg's murder. Burgee confessed to attempting to carjack Mrs. Shattenberg's rental car. Mrs. Shattenberg reportedly fought Burgee. DNA evidence confirmed Burgee's link to the crime. Burgee is currently serving a life sentence in Altwater State Correctional Facility in Illinois. Mrs. Shattenberg is survived by her husband, Solomon, an insurance claims investigator, and her two daughters, Samantha and Sophia, of Queens.

It had been so long since she'd disappeared, but in some ways it felt like it had just happened. Sometimes when the phone rang, I still thought that it might be her, and once I saw a woman in Bloomingdale's who looked just like her. I followed the woman as she wound her way through Home Furnishings until I got a good look at her face. It wasn't my mom, but a part of me couldn't help but hope that my mom was out there, somewhere, and might still come back, even though I knew that was impossible.

Right after she disappeared, we'd spent a week in Indianapolis looking for her. I kept thinking that I saw her all the time then—on line at the bank, in our hotel lobby, walking down every street. Our father went back to Indiana eleven times, but we never found more information about her. As an insurance claims investigator, he tried to use all his detective skills to try to find her on his own—interviewing people and digging up information. But he found nothing until the murderer was discovered in Chicago. Burgee had been picked up for another carjacking, and the police found evidence linking him to our mother's murder.

At least with our father we knew exactly what happened. At least before we'd gone to sleep that night, he'd told us he loved us and we'd told him we loved him, like we always did—we must've said it a dozen times a day, on the phone, in e-mails, in the morning, and before bed—as if we were always afraid one of us might disappear suddenly, too.

Even though they'd finally solved our mom's case, a part of me still wondered if I might see her again. I couldn't help it. A part of me had always sort of longed to go back to Indiana, thinking that we still might see her, though another part of me knew that wouldn't happen.

I finally mustered up the courage to ask Sam, "Did you decide on Indiana because of Mommy?"

"No," she said. She sounded annoyed. She didn't like talking about our mom that much. She didn't like that I'd made the scrapbook. She thought it was morbid and pointless.

"It's only because that's where Felix's contact is," she said. "And we've been there before, so we know it a tiny bit. It seems like a good place for us to go."

During our one week in Indiana we'd been so surprised by how different it was from anything we knew. I'd never really left New York City before, except for our two-week family vacations to Fire Island, which was only a couple hours away. I'd known that other big cities were smaller than New York, but I hadn't realized they were that much smaller. Indianapolis's small cluster of skyscrapers had looked so lonely and isolated, like a small slice of Manhattan. I kept expecting to see the rest of the buildings and skyscrapers evolve into more endless sprawling city, like New York, but twenty minutes out of the city all I saw was corn. Corn, corn, and more corn.

And I guessed I could expect to see more corn again soon. I sank down in the passenger seat of Felix's clunker car and watched the signs go by out the window for towns in New Jersey—Oldwick, Little York, Asbury—and then Pennsylvania. Maxatawny, Grimville. I still thought that Sam was somehow drawn to Indiana because of our mother. Sometimes I didn't totally understand Sam. She didn't like to talk about our mom or anything remotely having to do with her death, yet here we were now, on our way to Indiana.

I fell asleep somewhere in western Pennsylvania; I woke up in Ohio and rubbed my eyes. Fast-food signs dotted the horizon as well as a huge, gigantic cross in the distance. "Where are we?"

"A half hour past Dayton. We're about an hour or

two from Indianapolis. I'm not sure where we should stop, though."

"Aren't you exhausted?" I asked. "Do you want me to drive?"

"Um, *no*."

I was still too young to get a permit in New York City—you had to be sixteen—but my dad had spent several weekends giving me driving lessons in our car.

"You can drive when you get a little more experience," Sam said. "The last thing we need right now is to get pulled over for swerving or something."

"I don't swerve."

She raised her eyebrows. "And that time Daddy let you drive in Forest Hills, when you took out the hedge?"

"Oh yeah." I'd forgotten about that.

Soon we crossed over into Indiana. It was sunny and hot, around 5 P.M. now. We started seeing signs for a town called Venice.

**COME SEE VENICE
EUROPE OF THE MIDWEST**

**Visit Venice
See Our Beautiful Canal**

VENICE, CITY OF ROSES, NEXT EXIT

"Let's stop here," I said.

She glanced at the clock. "Let's just go a little farther."

I shifted in my seat. "I'm starving. I need to stretch my

legs. And you need to sleep." Sam looked so tired, her skin was pale, and she had dark circles under her eyes. They looked particularly bad against her newly blond hair. Also, a part of me wasn't ready to return to Indianapolis again just yet, to see all those places we had seen, those streets we'd walked on and stores we'd looked in, searching for our mother. To dredge up all those old feelings, on top of everything we were dealing with now. I just wanted to have something to eat, then go to sleep.

"Please," I said.

"All right," she said. "We'll just stop for a little while."

Three

When I woke up the next morning, I thought for a second that I was in my old bed at home, with my stuffed animals around me and my father brewing coffee downstairs. "I got bagels!" he would say. Sesame bagels with cream cheese and lox and red onion. And knishes from Knish Nosh on Queens Boulevard—spinach and potato, my favorite.

But I wasn't at home. Instead I was staring at the orange-and-green wallpaper of Ye Olde Venice Inn, with Ed the polar bear tucked under my arm. After my mom died, it had taken years before I'd remember, in those first few seconds after waking up, that she was really gone. How long would it be before I'd realize, in those half-awake moments, that my dad was gone, too?

I glanced over at Sam. She was still sleeping. She'd been so tired after we ate dinner last night that we'd decided to get a hotel room.

I put on my slippers and peeked through the flowered curtain. There was a cornfield out the window, stretching as far as I could see.

"Oy," I said.

Sam pulled the covers up over her eyes. "What time is it?" she mumbled.

"Seven-thirty."

"Oh my God. We slept twelve hours?"

I nodded.

She turned over and half buried her face in the pillow. "I feel like I could sleep twelve more."

I jumped back on the bed. "This running-away business is pretty exhausting," I said. I actually had a little energy, though. All of a sudden I felt surprisingly okay about not being at home. I still felt bad about leaving before shiva was over, but I knew my dad would understand. It had somehow seemed more upsetting to wake up in our old house the last few mornings, expecting our father to still be alive and to instead face another day of teary phone calls, constant visitors, and maudlin sympathy cards. Here everything was different—the bright colors, the crisp smell of the white sheets, the cornfields and meadows. I heard mooing off in the distance. We certainly weren't in Queens anymore.

"We have to get moving," Sam said. "This Difriggio guy is expecting us."

"Can't we go have breakfast somewhere? There's a diner downtown—I saw it in one of the pamphlets. And we can go see the canal."

"We have to get back on the road. Maybe we can come back here later or something."

I contemplated my new blond hair color and mole-less cheek again in the rearview mirror while Sam checked out of the hotel and loaded her knapsack into the Buick. I was looking forward to finding out if blondes did have more fun. Sam turned the key in the ignition.

Nothing happened.

"Give it more gas," I said. "Felix said you have to juice it—"

"*I am.*"

Still nothing happened. She sighed, got out of the car, and lifted up the hood. She fiddled around with something, came back in the car, and tried again. Nothing. She fooled around with it for several minutes more, then finally slumped in her seat. "It's dead."

A half hour later, after unloading all of our stuff from the car into our hotel room, we were bouncing around in the front seat of a tow truck alongside Chester Jones, owner of the Venice Auto Hut.

"I've been running the Hut for almost fifty years," Chester said as he drove. He looked about as ancient as our car; he wore a grease-stained jacket and bifocals. "What brings you two girls to Venice?"

I let Sam answer. "Well, we thought we'd stop and see the canal," she said.

"Where you girls from?" Chester asked. "Your parents back at the hotel?"

We'd rehearsed our story during the drive—what we would tell people we met about who we were and where we came from. I was eager to see whether Sam could pull it off.

"We're from Cleveland, though we've kind of lived all over," she said. "Our parents were musicians—we grew up traveling everywhere with them. Unfortunately"— here she paused for dramatic effect—"our parents both passed away. . . . They were killed in a car accident just a month ago."

It sounded so pathetic, I wanted to cry myself. Chester looked sad.

"Well, I'm awful sorry to hear about that." We pulled into the Auto Hut. "You girls just make yourself right at home here while I fix your vehicle. I got doughnuts, I got orange juice, whatever you want."

I took a Bavarian crème and a jelly one out of the Joy-Ann Donuts box, and we sat down on a bench by the side of the garage. In Queens, I wouldn't have eaten a free doughnut without worrying there might be a razor blade stuck inside. But Chester seemed trustworthy.

"You were perfect," I told Sam, wiping jelly off the side of my mouth. "An Academy Award–winning performance."

She bit into a chocolate glazed. "I'm glad we decided on the musician thing." We'd picked that because traveling around would explain why we knew so much about New York, from visiting it so often, and why we didn't know that much about Ohio. She stared out at the short buildings of the garage, and the fields beyond that, and chewed meditatively. "It's hard to imagine that anyone could ever find us here."

"Not the greatest news," Chester said as he wiped his hands on a rag. "You threw a rod. It's going to take me a week or two to get the part. That's an old car you got there."

"A week or two? Isn't there some way you can get it quicker?" Sam asked.

He shook his head. "I'm real sorry. At least you're lucky to be stuck here instead of all the places you could be. Venice is a great city with fine cultural attractions. We've got the canal, as you know. It's real beautiful. And they put in a new pool over by the country club. There's apple picking—I think that's just in the fall, though. And the Rose Parade—that's in a few weeks. The RoseTran bus will take you around. I'll call Ethel and get her to make a stop here. I think you'll like Venice. It's a nice town. I've lived here sixty-two years, and hardly anything's changed. This is a place where you could settle down and never miss the rest of the world, never even remember it existed."

Chester called the bus service, and ten minutes later a RoseTran minibus picked us up in front of Chester's garage. It was completely pink, with a huge, long-stemmed red rose painted on the side. Ethel, the driver, wore a pink jacket and pink sunglasses with lenses the size of dessert plates. We paid our fifty-cent fares and looked around. Two elderly people were nodding off in the backseat, but the rest of the bus was empty.

"Where do you girls want to go?" Ethel asked.

"Downtown, I guess," Sam said.

Apparently the bus had an improvised route—since so few people rode it, Ethel explained, she made her scheduled stops a couple of times a day in between her coffee, lunch, and snack breaks, but the rest of the time she just picked up people when they called and took them where they wanted to go. It was sort of a bus-meets-taxi service.

She took us to what was apparently the downtown, featuring a town hall building, the Petal Diner, and one street lined with shops. The town square was at the top of the street; in the center of it stood a huge statue of a gondolier. Behind that lay a little park with a white gazebo. Beyond the gazebo a sign pointed to the canal.

We walked over to the canal's edge. Apparently Chester hadn't actually viewed the canal recently.

"I've never been to Italy," I said. "But I assumed there was actually water in the canals in Venice."

"I did, too," Sam said.

This one was bone-dry, strewn with litter and a small black stray cat. It reminded me a little bit of the subway tracks.

On a lamppost nearby someone had stuck a "Save the Canal!" poster, with a phone number and Web site that was accepting donations.

We ate lunch at the Petal Diner. We sat at the counter and ordered two cheeseburgers, fries, milk shakes, blueberry pie, and coffee—all for $3.95 each. You could barely even get a cappuccino for that in New York City.

"You ladies just visiting here?" the woman behind the counter asked as she poured our milk shakes. She had a mane of bright orange hair piled high on top of her head and green eye shadow stretching up to her brows. She wore a pink chiffon scarf and so much costume jewelry, it must have added ten pounds to her weight.

"We saw the signs for the canal," Sam said.

"Oh, those," she said. "We've been debating about taking those down for years. Kind of a letdown when you finally see the canal, isn't it?" She stuck out her hand. "I'm Wilda," she said.

"Yeah, short for *Wildabeast*," a disheveled-looking man muttered from a back booth.

She waved her hand at him. "That's Gus. He's grumpy 'cause I'm putting him on a diet. No more pie for him till he loses a good twenty. He can barely fit in that booth. So you girls are tourists, then?"

We nodded. Tourists sounded like a nice, happy, carefree thing to be.

"There's not really a lot to see here," she confided. "Some nice shops, though. And the nicest people in the world live in Venice. We're like one big family. Right, Gus?" she shouted to the corner.

He grumbled something unintelligible.

We stuffed ourselves with food until we couldn't eat another bite. After we paid the bill, Wilda pointed us in the direction of the jewelry store, Romancing the Stone, which she said was the best jewelry store in the Midwest. Next door to that was a shop called It's Christmas! which sold Christmas tree ornaments year-round.

"I dare you to go in and ask for a menorah," I told Sam.

She gave me a look. "What's a menorah, Fiona Scott?"

"Oh, brother." Our family had never been very religious—Sam and I were both bat mitzvahed, but we only went to temple once a year, on Yom Kippur. But there certainly weren't any It's Christmas! stores in our neighborhood in Queens.

We walked past Bertha Kirk Intimates, which sold bras and panties so large, I could've used them as bedsheets. We walked down a few side streets of the town, too, which had names like Horse Chestnut Road, Picadilly Lane, and Summer Street. The old Victorian houses were painted pink, purple, yellow, and blue, like Easter eggs.

Inside a yellow house was a shop called Wright Bicycles, Etc. The emphasis seemed to be on the *Etc.*: tchotchkes, knickknacks, and junk from everywhere crowded the shelves and floors—ceramic animals and cement gargoyles, old lamps, paintings, antique furniture, and pocket watches. Shelves of used books towered to the ceiling. A dark-haired guy who looked a little older than me was repairing something in the back. He smiled at us.

I wanted to stay and browse through the books, but Sam checked her watch and said, "It's getting late. We should wait for Ethel."

"I kind of like it here," I said as we walked to the bus stop. I loved the colorful houses and friendly people and how different it was from New York, or Indianapolis, or anywhere I'd ever been. "It's not such a bad place to spend a week."

Sam stared down at the bright grass as we cut across the town square. "I like it, too."

We'd never traveled much as a family—my mom had been afraid of flying (she only took the train or drove on business trips). After she died, my dad, Sam, and I had never taken a vacation by ourselves. I guess it just never seemed right to go off somewhere without her. Then along came Enid, who certainly never traveled— she saw no reason to leave New York City. She often said that she thought the rest of the country could disappear and no one would notice.

Indiana was the farthest from New York that Sam and I had ever been.

I stared at the town square and the white gazebo. We were starting our lives over in the same state where our mother's had ended. Life had a strange way of working out, that was for certain. I wondered if she was watching over us somehow—I'd often thought that even though she was dead, she was still looking out for us. Sometimes I thought I could even feel her presence, protecting us—maybe she'd led us to Felix and made that old car survive the trip here to Venice instead of breaking down on a deserted highway. Maybe she—and our dad now—would protect us from getting caught. Maybe it was only my imagination, thinking that they were watching over us—but a part of me deeply believed that they were.

It was easy to blend into Venice for the week. Wilda (we'd been eating at the Petal Diner almost every day) put us in touch with Celeste, an elderly lady who rented a small, furnished house to us by the week—it was cheaper than the motel and just two blocks from downtown. It was a beautiful pink Victorian cottage with a front porch and two floors. I couldn't believe that we had the whole house to ourselves. It wasn't even attached to any other house, like our house in Queens was. We had a small yard, and hanging planters of pink petunias on the porch, and a porch swing. Inside, the furniture was all painted wood, old and colorful—red dressers and yellow bed frames and a bright blue kitchen table. The couches and beds were covered with beautiful quilts Celeste had made herself. There was an ancient thirteen-inch TV in the living room, connected to an equally old VCR. I was perfectly happy to just hibernate there and relax while Sam and I waited for our car to be ready.

Chester fixed our car as quickly as he could, and six days after it had broken down, we were at last on our way to see Difriggio. We'd called Difriggio from the cell phone Felix had given us and told him of the car predicament as soon as it happened. He'd said not to take the bus to see him—it was a little too public, he warned—before we'd been given our full instructions on how to keep our cover. Plus we'd be carrying a whole lot of money with us. So he'd advised us to hold off on the visit until we could make the trip by car.

My chest felt like I'd just swallowed a boulder as we drove into the city—I wasn't sure what I was expecting—some sign of my mother? But as we drove down the highway, the city looked different from the way I'd remembered it. It was sunny and clear, and the buildings looked bright and almost welcoming, so unlike the gloomy, dark, threatening place it had become in my memory.

Difriggio's headquarters were in a red-brick building that also housed a pizza place, a pool hall, and a tattoo parlor. He met us in the pool hall. He wore dark jeans and a white button-down shirt; his black hair peeked out from under his Yankees cap. He looked to be in his forties, though there was something young and boyish about him. His eyebrows were as thick as ferrets, and occasionally they wiggled when he spoke.

"I finally get to meet you," he said, and shook both our hands. "The Scott girls. Welcome." It was comforting to hear his Brooklyn accent—it had only been a week or so since I'd heard a real New York accent, but it felt like forever.

He led us through several winding corridors and into a private elevator in the back, which had letters instead of numbers on the buttons. He pushed *S,* and we were soon in a room with a shiny red floor and a stately wood desk. Framed black-and-white photos of what I assumed were his ancestors lined one wall; beneath them stood a row of square tables covered with red-checked tablecloths. On the opposite wall was a floor-to-ceiling painting of a dark-haired woman draped in a sheer toga, leaving little to the imagination. Potted palms dotted the corners, and behind one palm a sign on a door read, JACUZZI. The whole decorating scheme at work seemed to be Playboy-Mansion-meets-Ray's-Pizza.

Sam and I sat down on an antique sofa trimmed with gold-colored fabric.

"Felix is a good guy, isn't he? I taught him everything he knows. He learns quick," Difriggio said, reclining in his chair.

I was a little nervous in his office; I could tell Sam was, too. But at least it didn't look like the criminal hideout I'd imagined. As soon as he sat down at his desk, a huge orange tabby cat that must have weighed twenty pounds jumped on his lap with a thud. The cat purred so loudly, it sounded like a coffee grinder.

"Meet Cubby," Difriggio said. He waved one of Cubby's paws at us. Four pictures of Cubby were framed around his desk, and a copy of *Cat Fancy* lay on the filing cabinet. At least Difriggio seemed to be a criminal with a soft side. Not that I'd known any other master criminals in my time, but I'd never pictured them as subscribing to *Cat Fancy*.

Difriggio opened a pack of Juicy Fruit and offered us each a piece. We all sat there, chewing.

"So, Venice. It's not such a bad town for you to have ended up in. Maybe you should stick around there a little while. Lay low. I don't think anyone's going to look for you there. And there's a guy I know there, might be able to help you out."

"Who?"

"Let me contact him first. Hopefully you can settle in, not attract too much attention to yourselves, stay out of trouble. Do you like ravioli?"

Sam was about to shake her head, but I said, "I love ravioli."

"My nana makes it, sends it frozen. Mmm, you gotta try it." He picked up the phone, pressed an extension number, and said, "Artie, bring me up the Gorgonzola, for three."

Fifteen minutes later steaming plates of Gorgonzola ravioli with tomato sauce were served to all of us. We moved to the red-checked tables to eat. Difriggio tucked his linen napkin into his shirt. The ravioli was delicious—it was the best meal I'd eaten all week.

After he cleared his plate, Difriggio took off his nap-kin, and we returned to the sofa. He handed us two pieces of paper. "One thing you should be aware of. These were posted on-line."

They were two missing person's Web pages.

Sam looked them over first, then glared at me. "So someone did see you getting in the car," she said angrily. She shook her head.

I read them. "Well, someone saw you at the bank! That's even worse!"

"Ladies, ladies," Difriggio said. "Let's keep it together. It's not such a big deal yet. Felix has checked it out a little, and what's her name—the, uh, stepmother"—he glanced at the flyers—"Enid Gutmyre, now that's a charming name. Enid apparently thinks you're still in the city some-where and planning to head to Mexico or South America."

Sam looked proud of herself. "I left travel brochures for Mexico and Brazil in the garbage. And I packed all the photos of us so Enid wouldn't have access to them."

Difriggio nodded. "Good job. Maybe I'll be working for *you* someday." He scratched Cubby behind her ears. "What the police are doing right now is talking to your friends, your schoolteachers, your neighbors, the guests at your father's funeral—I'm really sorry about that, girls, by the way—friends of your dad's, anyone who could get a lead on you or who might know where you've been hiding."

I felt a huge pang, thinking about Viv. I couldn't

believe I hadn't even gotten to say good-bye to her. She had no idea where I was. She was probably really worried, especially if the cops were questioning her. I longed to call her up and tell her about Wilda, Chester, and our new house. She wouldn't believe that I was blond now and sitting here in the middle of Indiana, in the lair of a feline-obsessed major criminal. But I knew it was better for her not to know anything that was going on with me.

"Enid's putting more effort into the search for you than the police are—she put these reports together," Difriggio said. "I checked the police entries on the NCIC, and those were pretty basic. They have no idea where you are."

"NCIC?"

"National Criminal Information Center. It's a database that includes reports of missing persons across the country. But just a quick entry has been entered in New York City—no photo of you, nothing; the police here won't have your pictures, though if anyone finds out your real names, you're in huge trouble. You gotta be safe. Don't ever let it slip out. No calls, e-mails, letters, no contact at all with your friends in New York, nothing. You can't be in touch with anybody. Except Felix, who's got his back covered—but be careful even with that. You've disappeared, and what you've got to do now is set up your new life and blend into this town as if everything is perfectly normal."

"We're not ever going back, then?" My voice cracked, and a sob sneaked out. A part of me had known Sam hadn't been telling the truth when she'd said that we'd be able to go back sometime. But it made me sick to think about not ever seeing Viv again or seeing our house or anything familiar, ever.

Difriggio handed me a tissue. "It's possible you can, down the road. What you're up for is grand larceny, second degree. Class-C felony. CPL section 30.10 2(b) gives you a five-year statute of limitations. When that runs out, you might be able to go back. In the meantime you just gotta get settled here. It's not so bad. I love it. I don't miss Brooklyn at all, except for my nana, and the Yankees, and Patsy's Pizza, of course. You should try the pizza downstairs—good, but no Patsy's. It's something in the Brooklyn water makes the pizza taste so good."

"Can't I just send my best friend an e-mail?" I asked.

"No. No contact," Difriggio said. "You have to remember that. Or you could lose everything—I'm talking juvenile detention and prison here. You've committed fraud and major theft. No matter what, you'd be separated from each other, which according to Felix is exactly what you're working so hard to avoid here, right?"

I nodded, then blew my nose into the tissue. He handed me another one.

"I think we've been blending into Venice pretty well," Sam told him, clearly trying to lighten the mood. "We got a temporary apartment, and people have been friendly to us."

"Sounds good. See how you like Venice—I think it could be the perfect place for you to stay. No one's gonna find you there. Try to get settled, see what you think. Give it a couple of months. You should get yourselves some summer jobs. It'd help you both blend into the community even more." He leaned back in his chair; Cubby rested her head on his knee and blinked at us slowly. "And you might try to lose those accents a little."

"What accents?" Sam and I said, practically in unison.

"Believe me, I didn't think I had one, either," he said—even though he had one of the thickest Brooklyn accents I'd ever heard. "But you gotta watch it here if you want to blend in. Watch those New York words, too—*schlepp,* words like that—people here won't know what you mean."

We said we'd work on it. Sam told him the story we'd concocted about our parents, and he got on the phone to his assistant Artie and had him draw up a Cleveland Symphony poster and several sample playbills for concerts that our parents' chamber music ensemble had given around the country—things that would be good for us to have around our house. He even said he'd get some "notes dropped on the Web"—references to our fictional parents and their deaths, in case anyone in Venice wanted to check up on us on the Internet.

"These little things make a difference in making your story seem like the truth. And all the things you have that could possibly reveal your true identities— those have to be gotten rid of."

"I can't," I said. I had to stand my ground on this one. To get rid of these things—the only things we had of our parents—was impossible. "I'd rather get caught than throw it all out," I said. "I'm not going to do that, no matter what."

Difriggio paused. "All right, all right. I lost my mom

and pop, too, you know." He scratched Cubby, and she turned over, baring her belly. "What you do, then, is carve out someplace in the house, maybe under some floorboards, or hollow out the inside of a hassock. Hide the stuff there, and never, never take it out when anyone else is around. Clear?"

"Clear," I said.

He gave us our new birth certificates and Social Security cards. I stared at my birth certificate and then Sam's. I'd never looked closely at her new driver's license—according to her new birth certificate, she was twenty-one instead of seventeen, but my age was still the same. I pointed this out.

"Well, she has to be your legal guardian, and it just makes everything easier if she's twenty-one. You—why do you want to be any older? I'd give anything to be fifteen again." He stood up; Cubby jumped onto the floor and started rubbing against my ankles.

"I'm here for you, girls, whenever you need me. Or if you just want to shoot some pool and talk Yankees. You like the Yankees, I hope?"

"Of course," Sam said, as if even thinking she'd like another team was a personal affront.

"You're from Queens, so you could be Mets fans," Difriggio said.

"Our dad was a Yankees fan," Sam explained.

Difriggio smiled and patted our backs. He walked us to the elevator. We were going to hang out at the pizza parlor downstairs until Artie was done with our posters.

"Good luck, girls," Difriggio said.

"Thanks so much. I don't know what we would've done without your help, here and through Felix in New York," Sam said. She handed him an envelope, which I assumed was filled with a large wad of cash.

"Anytime," he said, setting the envelope on top of *Cat Fancy*. "Now go on downstairs until Artie gets you. Then go home and watch your backs."

Four

Sam and I were both jumpy over the next few days—whenever we heard wind in the trees in our garden or someone walking behind us, we'd tense up and get ready to run, afraid it might turn out to be Enid or the police. I wanted to trust Difriggio's advice that Venice was a good place for us to hide out, but somehow knowing that we had arrived at our permanent destination was unnerving.

On Monday afternoon we stopped in Wright Bicycles, Etc., to get a bike that I could ride to work. Getting jobs had been pretty simple: during breakfast at the Petal Diner, Ethel the bus driver had told us that the Rose Country Club was hiring, and that morning Sam had applied for a secretarial job in the front office and I'd applied to work at the concessions stand by the pool. Apparently the positions had been open for a while, with few applicants, because that afternoon we got a call from the club saying we were hired. They wanted us to start as soon as possible—we agreed to begin the next day.

Sam had to be there at eight, but I didn't have to be in until ten. "You have to get a bike," she said as we opened the door to the shop, "because there's no way I'm going to even try to get you out of bed at seven."

Lately I'd been going to sleep after David Letterman and waking up at the end of *Good Morning America*.

The dark-haired guy was in the back of the shop again, messing around with a unicycle. We browsed through the used books—the poetry section covered the entire side of one wall. I picked up an old, tattered copy of the *Collected Poems of Edna St. Vincent Millay*. My mom had a well-worn copy of that in our house in Queens—it was one of the books I hadn't been able to fit. Now I wished I had brought it. My stomach ached, thinking of everything we'd left behind. I fingered the cover.

"'Women have loved before as I love now,'" a male voice said behind me.

I turned around. "What?"

It was the bike guy. "That's a poem in there." He blushed slightly.

"Oh! I know." I smiled. "I love that poem."

He stuck out his hand. "I've seen you around here. You just moved into Celeste's house. I help Celeste out with that place—do just small repairs and maintenance and stuff."

"You're Colin?" I asked. "Celeste gave us your number to call if we needed anything fixed." Looking around his shop, I could see the same bright colors of the antique painted furniture in our house.

He nodded. There were supposedly fifteen thousand people living in Venice and the surrounding area, but it felt like such a tiny town. Everyone seemed to be connected.

"I'm Sophie," I said, "and this is my sister, Sam."

Sam shook his hand, too. "Have you lived here your whole life?" Sam asked him.

"Yeah—I've traveled a lot, though," Colin said. "My dad's a lawyer and isn't here much—he's in London right now, on business for two months. I've gone away with him before, but I like staying here and running the shop. And he trusts everyone around town to keep an eye out for me—believe me, the people here are more than happy to oblige. Gives them something to do, although it's not like they'd ever discover anything too exciting."

I shot Sam a worried glance. Nosy townspeople were the last thing we needed. But hopefully Difriggio was right that we'd be safe in Venice.

Colin told us he was sixteen and would be a junior at Venice High in the fall—a year ahead of me. His dark brown bangs kept falling onto his wire-rimmed glasses. His jeans and black T-shirt had smears of blue and yellow paint across them.

"Venice is a quirky old town. It was founded by an Italian guy over a hundred years ago, but the canal didn't get built till the 1970s—it was supposed to make this place a tourist attraction. Unfortunately, that didn't really work."

"The canal does seem a bit on the dry side," I said.

He grinned. "So is there anything you're looking for?" He glanced around the shop.

"Actually, we're looking for a bike for Sophie here," my sister said.

"I just want something small so it's not too far to the ground when I fall off," I said.

The embarrassing fact was, I didn't even know how

to ride a bike. I'd tried to a few times in New York, but the sidewalks around our house were always so crowded, and it was too dangerous to ride in the street. Sam assured me it wasn't hard. She'd braved the crowded sidewalks and the city streets to teach herself when she was little, but I'd never been that gutsy about it.

"I just never learned," I said, and shrugged. I hoped not everyone in Cleveland knew how to ride a bike.

He shuffled through some papers behind the cash register and handed a pamphlet to Sam. "Read this— it's really great." It was called "Teach Your Child to Ride a Bike."

I shook my head. This was slightly mortifying.

Colin led us out back, and I tried sitting on different bikes. He was quiet for a minute; he put his hands in his pockets and leaned against what looked like a rusted piece of farm equipment. "Celeste told me about your parents. I'm really sorry." I looked at Sam—news traveled fast in this place. But he seemed more sincere than most people who say they're sorry—usually it sounded automatic and kind of meaningless, but somehow his voice made it sound real. "My mom died, too, three years ago," he said.

There's an instant connection and understanding when someone tells you their mom or dad has died, too. An unspoken bond; they know what it's like. I figured that was why Difriggio was helping us out—when I'd questioned Sam about how much cash was in that envelope she gave him, she'd said he was giving us a reduced rate. I wondered if we were drawn to people who had lost parents now—or if they were drawn to us.

Sam's face relaxed, and her voice softened. "I'm sorry," she told Colin.

"Me, too," I said.

He shrugged and stared at the bike I was sitting on—a little red Schwinn with a blue basket in front. "Do you like that one?"

I rang the bell on the handlebars. "I love it."

He wheeled it toward the front of the shop and said, "Let me know if there's anything else you need or if you want help settling in . . ."

"Thanks," Sam said. "I think we're okay, though."

The bells on the shop door jingled, and a middle-aged woman walked in. She wore a gray suit. She was the first older woman I'd seen in Venice who wasn't wearing anything pink. "Hi, Nancy," Colin said. The woman—Nancy—gave him a smile and a nod and then poked around the store for a few minutes. She finally bought a handkerchief, an antique cameo bookmark, and a little ceramic cow.

"Nancy, let me introduce Sam and Sophie Scott," Colin said. "They just moved here. Nancy's the mayor of Venice."

"Oh, wow," Sam said. "It's great to meet you." My sister and I exchanged looks. We'd definitely never seen Rudy Giuliani just wandering into stores and hanging out, back when he'd been mayor of New York.

"Nice to meet you, too." The mayor flashed another quick smile, seeming a little rushed. "I guess I'll just take these."

Colin started to add up her items on a handwritten

receipt. The mayor said not to bother. She just paid, then put the items in a small bag and hurried off.

"I can't believe the mayor just wanders into your shop like that," I said.

Colin stashed the receipt below the cash register. "Well, this isn't Cleveland. I hope you enjoy it, being in a smaller town."

"It's a big change from Cleveland," Sam agreed. "But so far we really like it."

We paid for the bike and the Edna St. Vincent Millay book. "I hope you'll come stop by anytime," he said. He smiled at me. "Good luck with learning to ride. Let me know if you need any pointers."

"I will," I said.

As I wheeled the bike back to our house (I wasn't ready to hop on it just yet), I said to Sam, "So, I guess we're going to stay here for a little while."

She picked a honeysuckle bloom off a bush as we walked by. "Difriggio seems to think it's a good place for us. Honestly, I wasn't sure exactly where we'd end up. But it's not so bad here, is it? Maybe it was sort of serendipity that we found this place."

"Maybe. I kind of like it. The people are so friendly. And I like Celeste's house."

"Good," Sam said. "Then I guess we'll stay, at least for a while, and see how it goes."

I wanted to tell her what I really felt—how much I just wanted to go back home. Not home as we left it—but our old home, with our dad there and my friends nearby. I had to keep reminding myself that our old life didn't exist anymore and wouldn't have existed for me even if we'd stayed in New York.

The learning-to-ride-a-bike thing didn't go so well, and I ended up walking the two miles to the club the next morning. It was an especially hot day, and I was sweaty and cranky by the time I got to work. Why couldn't we have run away to some place that wasn't just as sticky and humid as New York?

It was a pretty dull job—pouring sodas, which everyone called "pop," melting cheese on top of nachos. I had to wear a frilly pink apron and a rose-shaped button imprinted with HI! MY NAME IS FIONA. There was a little kitchen in the back where Henry, my boss, flipped burgers, boiled hot dogs, defrosted frozen pizza, and fried fries. I added the condiments and served. The food was greasy and nowhere near as good as the hot dogs in New York. And Henry wasn't very open to my suggestions for improvement.

"We could serve knishes," I suggested.

"K-whats?"

"Knishes? You know—potato, spinach, and stuff?"

"Never heard of them."

"Oh," I said. "They make really good ones in Cleveland."

I longed to drive with my dad the fifteen minutes to Knish Nosh and get a knish right now. Or to walk to Turkiyem on the corner of Forty-seventh Street with him and get one of those amazing Turkish spinach pastries they sold there. Or go to Sunny Grocery and buy real baklava. Or we could get a sweet red bean bun at the Chinese bakery. I missed all those places. I'd never even appreciated them until we'd landed here, in uniformly white Venice. I hadn't seen a single person in this town yet who wasn't thoroughly, 100 percent cornbelt white—and I hadn't found anything but totally midwestern food.

"Stop thinking about kerfishes, Fiona, and put the ketchup on that order," Henry barked.

"It's Sophie," I said, for what seemed like the hundredth time.

"Whatever." Henry was only a couple of inches taller than me but about a hundred pounds heavier and one of the hairiest people I'd ever seen. Even his feet were hairy, which I'd had the misfortune to notice when he'd donned his turquoise swimming trunks and belly flopped into the pool.

It certainly wasn't very glamorous work, but at least the pool was beautiful, and we were allowed full use of it as well as the hot tub. It was peaceful to just hang out behind the cash register and look at the water and blue sky. But sometimes a kid would come up to the counter and say, "Two Pepsis and a large fries, please," and I wouldn't even hear him. I'd be off in another world in my head. I'd be back in New York City on the number 7 train with Viv. We'd be talking about Mr. Platek, our math teacher, who all the girls had crushes on. Then we'd be at my house, making my mother's famous blueberry blintzes, and my dad would say they were as good as hers.

"Lady, are you okay?" A ten-year-old boy was looking up at me.

"Oh, I'm fine." I wiped a tear out of the corner of my
eye. "What was your order?"

I soon learned that the best part of my new job was
gazing at the lifeguard. He sat perched over the pool in
his little white tower. He had pale blond hair—even
lighter than Ivory Moon—and wore no shirt. His chest
and stomach muscles reminded me of the guys in the
Calvin Klein underwear ads in Times Square. Before
lunch he came over to me and asked for a Sprite.

"I see something beautiful has arrived," he said.

At first I thought he meant a fancy car or something,
and I actually glanced over at the parking lot—then I
realized he was eyeing me. I stared at him awkwardly,
not knowing what to say.

He glanced at my name tag. "Hello, Fiona. I'm Troy
Howard."

"People call me Sophie, actually. Troy—as in Helen of?"

"Huh?" He looked at me quizzically.

"The Greek myth? You know—Homer?"

"Oh yeah," he said, though I don't think he knew
what I was talking about. I stood there trying to think of
something to say, staring at his tan and muscular chest.

Before I could come up with anything, a tall, thin,
bronzed girl with silky straight blond hair came up to
us. She wore a pink bikini top and denim shorts.

"I see you've met the new girl, Troy," she said. She
turned to me. "We haven't been introduced. I'm Noelle."

"Nice to meet you," I said.

She smiled fakely. Her teeth were so white, I wanted to put on my sunglasses. "Lacey has something she needs to ask you," she said to Troy, and led him off toward her group of friends.

At lunchtime Sam and her boss from the front office, Fern, came out for hot dogs. Fern was about Wilda's age—somewhere in her fifties—and seemed to go to the same hairstylist, since her dark brown hair was piled above her head in a similar mountainous 'do. She wore rhinestone glasses and a sundress covered with smiling poodles.

"Have you met the other girls your age here yet?" Fern asked.

"Just Noelle," I said.

Fern shook her head. "Noelle McBride is a piece of work. The other girls are nicer."

After lunch Fern took us to the other side of the pool and introduced us to Lacey, Tara, and Claire—they were sitting around Noelle under a table with an umbrella. Each of them wore a lavender string bikini, and matching cutoff pink T-shirts with PRINCESS emblazoned across the front. They eyed me and Sam as if we were specimens in biology class.

I figured I'd just wait till the fall to make some friends. I couldn't imagine myself fitting in with girls who wore matching pink princess T-shirts. I was used to fitting in at La Guardia, my high school—though there you could have blue hair and twelve cheek piercings and still fit in. In the meantime, there was Troy to occupy my thoughts. Staring at him certainly made my workday go faster.

Toward the end of the afternoon Noelle, Lacey, Tara, and Claire got on the concessions line; they ordered nachos without cheese and four iced coffees.

All four of them were at least six inches taller than me. What did they feed these girls in the Midwest? Was there something in the corn?

"No milk or sugar for us. I have to fit into that leotard for the Rose Parade," Tara said.

"What's the Rose Parade?" I asked. "I think I heard something about it."

They looked at me like I was crazy. "It's only the biggest event of the year," Tara said.

"And you're looking at the Rose Queen," Noelle said.

Lacey, who was standing behind Noelle, rolled her eyes. Her blond hair curled up and out at the ends, like a wig from the sixties.

Their order came up, and I placed the food on the counter. "One order of nachos without cheese and four iced coffees, all black," I said.

"*Cawfees?*" Lacey repeated, mimicking me. "Where are you from?"

I could feel my face redden. I'd been trying to lose my accent, like Difriggio had said—but that was hard to do when I didn't even think I had much of one in the first place. "I'm from Cleveland," I said.

"I *thought* that was a Cleveland accent," Noelle said.

"My uncle's from Cleveland, and he doesn't sound

like her," Claire said. She wore her dark hair in a long ponytail; she kept twirling the end of it.

Noelle eyed me up and down. "You don't get out much, do you? I've never seen skin so pale."

"Oh, I wear sunscreen," I said.

"And what on earth are you wearing on your feet?" Noelle asked, staring down at my extra-thick-soled Steve Madden platform sandals. My favorite shoes. They made me about three inches taller. Viv had helped me pick them out.

I tried to ignore Noelle and just wiped off the counter.

"I guess you need them when you're a dwarf," Noelle said, and her friends giggled.

I could feel my face flush. How was she managing to zero in on everything that I was sensitive about? I hadn't been picked on this much since Evelina Gosmelder at Mid-Queens Day Camp when I was ten. Evelina had been able to make me cry in less than two minutes.

I tried to think of what to say as I cleaned the counter, hoping they'd just walk away. But Noelle added loudly, "As Rose Queen, I'm going to do my best to help Venice's underprivileged residents. The dwarves, the pasty, the orphans."

I stared at her. Had she really just said that? Hearing the word *orphan* come out of her mouth made me feel slightly dizzy and sick. Sometimes lately, when I'd thought of that word, I'd think, *That can't be me*. It was such an awful word in so many ways, so sad and pathetic, like I should have had coal-dusted cheeks and been asking for more porridge. We'd had parents, and they'd loved us. They just hadn't lived as long as most people's did.

I didn't know what to say. Finally I blurted, "At least . . . at least I'm not . . . a Hoosier!"

As soon as the words were out of my mouth, I realized how ridiculous they sounded. A Hoosier wasn't even an insult; it was what people from Indiana called themselves. The girls looked at me like I was insane.

"What a loser," Noelle said, and shook her head as they walked away.

I put my rag down on the counter and retreated to the back, behind the deep-fat fryer, trying really hard not to start crying. I thought if I did, I'd never stop.

"Good to see you're making friends," Henry said.

I didn't tell Sam about the Noelle episode. She seemed so happy after her day, and I figured she'd be angry if she knew I'd called Noelle a Hoosier, no matter how pathetic an insult it was. We hadn't even been in the town two weeks, and already I had an enemy.

"The country club is a perfect place for us to work because everyone from town comes through there," Sam said. "We'll be able to tell if anyone gets suspicious of us. And Fern really likes us."

"Yeah, that's great," I said weakly.

We walked from our house to the Petal Diner. I was looking forward to drowning my sorrows in food.

"Look, it's the working girls. Have I got a meal for you!" Wilda said to us as we entered. "Chicken-fried steak. You ever have chicken-fried steak?"

I'd never even heard of such a thing.

She served it to us: it was exactly what it sounded like, as if someone had slipped a sirloin into KFC batter. It actually tasted wonderful.

Apparently a large portion of town had been alerted to the fact that it was chicken-fried-steak night because Chester, Ethel, and Fern showed up that night, too.

"Heard you girls are working at the Rose Club," Chester said. "I just might come by and pay you a visit. Been years since I've been in that pool." I tried not to picture him in a bathing suit.

Fern brought her dog, Isabel, a standard poodle. Apparently Isabel was also fond of chicken-fried steak.

"That dog eats better than I do," Ethel said as Fern fed Isabel half of her biscuit.

For dessert Wilda gave us all slices of chocolate fudge cake for free. Well, all of us except for Gus, who was moping in a booth in the back. We hadn't seen him in the diner for the last few days—Wilda explained that he'd defected from her place to go splurge at Hardee's and Dairy Queen.

He argued with Wilda to give him a slice of cake, but she remained firm. "I let you have that chicken-fried steak, and that was enough. Anyway, I just gave away the last piece."

She went back to the kitchen, and I could feel Gus's eyes on us. Or more specifically, on our cake. "I'm going to give him a little bit," I told Sam. I cut my piece in half and put part on a napkin. "He's not that fat."

I brought it to his booth. "Thank you," Gus said. "You just made my night."

"Diets are no fun," I said.

"I'm not on a diet. That's Wilda's idea. She likes to mother me. But I say, if it ain't broke, why fix it?" He gobbled the cake in two bites.

"What's his story?" I asked Wilda later.

"Oh, he's been this way ever since his wife left him," she said. "Drinks too much, eats too much . . ." She shook her head. I stared at him. He looked lonelier and worse off than we were.

When we couldn't eat another bite, Wilda wrapped up extra pieces of chicken-fried steak for us to take to work the next day, and Chester and Ethel congratulated us on our new jobs. Fern gave us a big hug and said she'd see us tomorrow. Wilda had been right about Venice—the people here seemed like some of the nicest I'd ever met. That is, if you didn't count Noelle.

Five

Henry was teaching me how to use the cappuccino machine when I looked up and saw Troy at the counter. He had his dog with him, a little brown-and-white beagle.

He ordered a Häagen-Dazs ice-cream bar. It was ten-thirty in the morning.

"Ice cream for breakfast?" I said.

He smiled. "Starts the day off right. This is Fonzie." His dog leaped up toward the counter.

"Hey, Fonzie," I said.

Troy paid for the ice-cream bar and put a dollar in the tip jar. "Are you going to karaoke tonight?" he asked me. There had been signs up around the country club advertising it—apparently it was a regular tradition. I'd tried not to pay too much attention, though. Thinking about singing made something kind of sink inside me because I missed it so much.

"I don't know," I said. "I've never been to karaoke before." Then it hit me—was he asking me out? Was the handsomest guy in town actually interested in me? Maybe my mom really *was* watching over me. This was certainly the best thing to happen to me in weeks.

"You should come," Troy said. "You'll like it."

"Well . . . okay."

"Great. So I'll see you there, Fiona."

"Sophie."

"See you there, Sophie." He gave me another smile, then walked away. Fonzie trotted off after him.

The countertop in front of me dazzled. Light bounced off the soda machine and the plastic cups. Even the lingering aroma of fried burgers suddenly smelled great.

At lunchtime Sam and Fern joined me to eat leftover chicken-fried steak. "Everyone goes to karaoke," Fern said. "It's the biggest thing to do around here, next to planning the Rose Parade. The only problem is hearing that one over there sing." She glanced at Noelle, on the other side of the pool.

"Sophie's got a great voice," Sam said. "You should hear her."

"We'll sign you up tonight," Fern said.

"I don't think so," I said. For some reason I just couldn't bring myself to sing or play music here in our new place. I guess it opened up a part of me where I wasn't ready to go right now—all those old emotions. Maybe I thought it would make me feel too much or something. I wasn't sure. I just didn't want to perform here, in front of strangers—especially in front of Noelle and her whole crew. Singing was the one thing I did that I wanted to keep to myself, to keep it sort of sacred.

"I mean—I want to go tonight, I just don't want to sing," I said.

"Well, maybe you'll change your mind. Especially after you hear Chester go through his rendition of

'Home on the Range.' We could use a new voice around here, let me tell you," Fern said.

It seemed like the entire town was filling the rec room of the country club, including everyone from work: Wilda, Gus, Ethel, Chester, Troy, Noelle and company, and even Celeste, the owner of our house.

Colin came over to Sam and me as soon as we entered the room, and we sat at a table together. "You both look nice," he said to us.

"Oh, thanks." I'd put my hair up with different clips in it. I was wearing a black flower-print halter dress and black strappy high heels (I'd decided against my platform shoes, after Noelle's comment). Sam wore her nicest black oxfords, jeans without holes in the knees (that was her version of dressing up), and a blue button-down shirt. After much nagging from me, she had agreed to stick a jeweled barrette in her short hair.

The lights were dimmed, and candles had been placed on all the tables. Henry had set out a bowl of punch on a table in the back of the room.

Colin pointed out the people at other tables who we hadn't met yet. "Those ladies over there in the red jackets are in the Rose Society. They plan the parade and are writing a Rose Petal cookbook. There's Greg, Noelle's ex. He's in a band, Dog Breath." Greg was wearing a studded black belt and a Megadeth T-shirt. I couldn't believe Noelle had gone out with him; he seemed like the polar opposite of Troy.

"There's Nancy Weller, the mayor—you met her,

remember?—and her husband, Bill. Then the next table over is the chief of police, Chief Callowe, and his brother, Officer Albert—everyone calls him Alby." I was afraid to even look at the chief and his brother—I wanted as little to do with them as possible.

"And there's Troy, the lifeguard—you've probably met him already."

"Oh yeah, I did," I said, trying to sound casual.

"And that fellow in the sparkly cowboy outfit is Johnny Parsons. He's from Nashville, but he's been hanging around here this summer. Apparently he comes here—believe it or not—to scout talent."

"Does he really think he's going to find new talent at karaoke night in Venice?" I asked.

"Maybe he'll discover you!" Fern interjected, and winked at me.

His jacket glittered in the light; I'd never seen so many sequins in one place. Maybe it was the jaded New York part of me, but he just didn't seem like any serious recording executive type I'd imagine. "I don't know if I'd want to be discovered by that guy," I said.

We watched Parsons open his wallet and take out several pictures, which were passed around the table of Rose Society ladies. They soon made their way to our table, too: they were of his pet squirrel—wearing, believe it or not, a neon-green collar that glittered like Parsons's jacket.

"Sparky had a big infection on the side of his face when I found him," Parsons explained to us as we looked at the pictures. "You can't even tell now."

There was a picture of Sparky wolfing down a plate of spaghetti.

"He only likes it with sauce. Prego with mushrooms and garlic, that's his favorite."

We passed the photos on to the next table.

"I know, it's not Cleveland," Colin said. "Venice attracts the strange ones, for some reason. Keeps things interesting, though." He introduced us to his friends from high school—Fred Lamb and Larry Jackson, and several others whose names I couldn't remember. None of them came by the pool in the afternoons.

The karaoke soon began, hosted by Bea Sellers, president of the Rose Society. She introduced the rest of the Rose Society ladies, who sang a squeaky rendition of "Stop! In the Name of Love." Then Bea introduced Noelle.

Fern was right. Noelle singing karaoke gave a new meaning to the word *torture*. Apparently she was on a Madonna kick, since she launched into a creatively disimpassioned version of "Don't Cry for Me, Argentina" and followed it up with "Beautiful Stranger." She seemed to think she sang wonderfully, though. She looked gleeful, posing with the microphone.

"Sophie, why don't you go up there?" Sam said.

"I don't think so."

Fern looked at me. "Oh, come on. Do it."

"We need to hear someone who can actually sing," Colin said.

I'd never done karaoke before, and it seemed a little strange to me. But it was when I looked over at Troy and our eyes met that I thought that I might try. I guess

I kind of wanted to prove something to Noelle. I know that wasn't the most noble of reasons, but after all of her comments to me, I needed to do something to show I wasn't such a loser. I knew this was one thing that I could actually do well.

I signed up on the sheet. I looked through the book of songs to sing and finally picked one. It was "Five Hundred Miles," which my mom used to sing to me. I was surprised that it was in there. We used to listen to it on my mom's Peter, Paul and Mary albums at home.

The karaoke went on for nearly two hours; I was one of the last people to sing.

"If you miss the train I'm on, you will know that I am gone," I began. My voice started out a little scratchy but in a second the song took over, and it was almost as if it started to sing itself. I stopped thinking about Venice and our dad and our new lives . . . I was just singing. When I got to the chorus—*"Lord, I'm five hundred miles from my home"*—I even felt sort of comforted . . . that I wasn't the only one to have gone through this, to have left home and started over.

"Wow," Fern said when I came back to my seat. "I've never heard anything so beautiful. Girl, you can really sing."

"She's right," Colin said.

Troy raised his root-beer bottle in my direction.

Sam looked uncomfortable. I'd thought she'd be happy with that song since the word *Lord* appeared in it repeatedly—it sounded Christian enough to me. But I knew that it probably reminded her of our mom, just like it did me. So much had happened recently; it was all so overwhelming, I couldn't even wrap my head around it. How had I ended up in this new life?

I sipped my punch, and then I went to the bathroom; I just wanted to have a few minutes alone to get myself together. But I was hardly in there a few seconds when Lacey and Noelle walked in. I stood at the mirror, reapplying my blush and lipstick.

"That was great," Lacey said.

Noelle gave her a stern look.

"Thanks," I said hesitantly, waiting for whatever comment would surely come next.

Noelle put on a coat of bright pink lipstick and then said, "I think next time you should do 'It's a Hard Knock Life.'"

I didn't respond. I couldn't believe that she'd just said that. What kind of a person would say something like that?

She murmured a bar from the song, off-key. *"When you're in an orphanage . . ."*

"What do you have against me?" I said. "I haven't done anything to you."

Lacey looked almost excited, as if she was about to witness a real catfight.

"I just want to make sure that the country club, for one thing, has people of the right *kind* working there. We don't want people from questionable backgrounds preparing our food, or lurking around the pool, or tormenting us with their hokey music."

I told myself to ignore her. I told myself to let it go.

"I heard your parents were musicians like you," she said.

I was too stunned to answer.

"Were they dwarves, too? Maybe that's what made people listen to them. A kind of freak-show thing."

Enough. "Why don't you think about how it would feel if *your* parents died in a car crash. Or if *you* did!"

I didn't realize I was yelling that loudly, but a couple of people poked their heads inside the bathroom to see what was going on. Noelle shrugged, gave a little laugh, and walked out, and I stood there, wanting to cry and feeling so angry that I couldn't. I stayed in there a few minutes until I got myself together. When I went back outside, Sam was seething. We walked behind the club until we were sure that we were far enough away that no one could hear us.

"Are you crazy? Do you remember the basic tenet we're supposed to follow? You know, the one that Difriggio told us—*do not draw attention to yourselves*?"

"I'm sorry, but that girl is insane. She's evil!" I told her what Noelle had said. "I mean, who would *do* that? Who would say that?"

"Sophie." Sam shook her head. She looked so disappointed. "You're right. She was totally out of line. But it's just—this is serious. You've got to be more careful."

"Okay. I know. I'm sorry."

"You have to tell Noelle that," she said.

"What?"

"That you're sorry."

"I'm not apologizing to Noelle," I said.

"I think you are."

"What are you saying? You know, you're not my mother."

Her face turned red. "There's only one way that we're going to survive, and that's if we blend in. If you want to make a mess of things, you're going to have to clean it up. Or we just might lose everything. *Apologize to Noelle.*"

I stared down at the grass, pushing a pebble with my toe. I thought she was taking this legal guardian thing a little too far; she'd always had her bossy-older-sister moments, but with this new power, it was getting a little hard to take.

She must have had an idea of what I was thinking because she added, "I'm not just trying to tell you what to do. Our lives could be at stake here." Her voice was beginning to break. "You have to smooth things over."

I relented. "Fine."

We asked Lacey where Noelle was, and Lacey said she was by the pool.

Sam and I started walking that way, and as we approached, we heard Noelle's voice, yelling. Apparently she was having a pretty busy night.

"You're such a bum! You think you're so great, but little do you know . . ." The rest was muffled. We heard a male voice, too—it was Troy's. We couldn't make out what he was saying until we heard him yell, "Well, good—*I've had enough of you!* I'm getting out of here."

Then Troy stormed by us.

A few seconds later Noelle walked by, too.

Sam nudged me.

"Um, Noelle," I called after her. She turned around. "I'm really sorry about the fight we had. I think it would be great if we could try to be friends." I tried to make my voice sound sincere—I thought of the exercises some of my friends in school did in acting class. I pretended Noelle was the evil queen and I, the noble young maid, had to be nice to her to get what I needed.

"Oh, please," Noelle said, and huffed off.

"Well, that was effective," Sam said.

I shrugged. "I tried."

Back in the rec room Noelle and Lacey had their jackets on and were sitting sulkily at a table. Tara and Claire had already left. The punch table was cleared, and all the tablecloths were put away. Everyone we knew was gone—including Troy.

"Colin was looking for you," Lacey told us. "I said I thought you'd already left." She stared at her feet. "Hey—are you guys driving home now?"

"Lacey, my parents will come get us *later*," Noelle told her.

"I'm not waiting another hour," Lacey said.

"You can get a ride with us," Sam offered. "No problem." She seemed eager to help them out, to make amends.

"My parents will *come*," Noelle said to Lacey, her voice firm.

Lacey grabbed her purse. "I'm tired, and I just want to go home. I'm going with them."

Noelle scowled, then gathered her own things and followed us to the car. I wanted to ask what had happened with Noelle and Troy but didn't think Sam would approve of the question.

When we reached our old brown car, Sam opened the passenger side for Noelle and she climbed in, banging her leg on the door as she did. "Ow," she grumbled. "This thing is like a rusty tin can."

"It's an old car," Sam explained.

"It should be put out of its misery," Noelle said.

Maybe you *should be put out of your misery,* I thought. I couldn't believe she was being this rude to Sam, too.

Noelle sulked quietly throughout the drive, picking lint off her skirt. Sam made a few attempts at conversation. "What do your parents do?" she asked Noelle.

"They own the *bank,*" Noelle said, as if she couldn't believe Sam didn't know.

"Oh," Sam said. "That's great." After a few minutes she added, "Venice is a really nice town."

Noelle sighed and turned toward the window. Thankfully, Lacey soon directed us toward a pretty brick house on a suburban-looking street, about five miles from where we lived.

"Thanks!" Lacey said; she shut the door and hurried up her driveway.

Noelle lived another mile farther. Her place was a huge white house with columns in front and manicured hedges lining the lawn. The windows were dark. She opened the car door, grabbed her purse, and closed the door without saying good-bye or thank you. We watched her run up the steps to her house, turn the key, and slam the door behind her.

Six

The next morning at the country club Lacey, Tara, and Claire sat by themselves under their usual umbrella. I kept waiting for Noelle to make her grand entrance later on in the day, as she often did, stripping off her shorts and T-shirt with a flourish to display her newest bikini. When she didn't show up in the afternoon, I thought maybe she'd been sick or had something to do, but I didn't really think about it too much. I was enjoying not having to worry what she was going to say to me the next time she got on the concessions line.

At the end of the day, when I looked into my mail slot in the club office, I found a little white envelope beside my time sheet. Inside the envelope was a gold necklace with a heart charm and a note.

FROM YOUR SECRET ADMIRER

I looked around the room. Was this really for me? Was it in the right mail slot? Could it be from (did I dare even think it?) Troy?

I put the necklace on and went over to Sam's desk. I waited for her to notice it as we got ready to leave the club. I kept fingering the heart charm, but she didn't seem to see it.

"Did you see Troy come by the office this afternoon?" I asked her.

She shrugged. "No."

"Do you like my necklace?"

"It's okay."

"It was a gift," I said.

"Oh, really?" she said without interest.

"I just found it in my mailbox."

She hovered over her desk, gathering her papers.

"I think it's from Troy!" I said, and showed her the note.

She shook her head. "Oh God. I should just keep you locked up in a shed, where you have no access to any boys."

"What should I do? I mean, it has to be from Troy. I think. Who else could it be from?"

She shook her head again. Ordinarily I never asked Sam for advice about my love life. I always called Viv. And right now, even though I knew I couldn't, I wanted desperately to take the cell phone away from Sam and sneak off somewhere to call Viv—to tell her about Troy and his blond hair and smooth chest. Neither Viv nor I had boyfriends at home, though one of us always seemed to have a new crush. Sam never admitted to even ever having had a boyfriend—she much preferred to devote all her time to physics class and math team.

"Of all the people you fall for here," Sam said, "why Troy? He's good-looking, yeah, but he has the brains of a mosquito. Have you actually said anything to him besides 'Here are your fries'? And anyway, he's Noelle's boyfriend."

"I don't think he's Noelle's boyfriend anymore. You heard them—I think they broke up last night."

"Even so, it's a little soon for him to be giving you jewelry. Maybe it's not even from Troy. Maybe it's from your boss, Henry."

I shuddered. Henry was more likely to give me a lump of coal than a necklace. "Very funny. I can guarantee you it's not from Henry."

We made our way to the parking lot, and Sam unlocked our car. "In any case, I don't think you should go out with anybody. We need to blend in—but not *that* much."

I ignored her, instead imagining Troy's tanned body arriving on our porch to pick me up, his blond hair falling into his eyes.

"Hello? Featherbrain? Have you been listening to anything I've been saying?"

"Yeah. Of course," I said.

"What did I say?"

"Um. The stock market went up today?"

She groaned. "What am I going to do with you? I was saying that they put a notice up on the Bronx Science Web site about me being missing. So thank God you didn't tell Viv where we were, because if she'd told her brother, word would've gotten around really fast, especially once school started up again."

Viv's brother, Kyung, went to the same high school as Sam. "She wouldn't have told anyone, though," I said.

"You don't know that for sure. All it takes is one person. Word could get around so easily."

"Maybe." I slumped in my seat, brought back to the

real world. I wished we could just live our lives like normal people and I could fantasize about handsome lifeguards in peace without having to worry about being arrested.

When we got home, Sam decided that I should practice bike riding again.

"I'm sick of it," I said. "I suck."

"You don't. You're making great progress."

This was definitely not true: I fell off every three seconds. Sam studied the pamphlet that Colin had given us. According to it, I was supposed to learn to "coast" first, which meant balancing and rolling along without pedaling. I tried this on our street, and it sort of worked: I cruised along cautiously, with Sam shouting encouraging comments behind me. We coasted by Colin's store, and he came out to say hi. Soon he and Sam were both shouting, "Way to go! You're doing great!" behind me, like two teenage parents. It was embarrassing.

Colin and Sam were still cheering for me when Colin's friend Fred Lamb stopped by the shop. He was a few inches taller than Colin, with bright red hair and jeans that were slightly too short.

"Did you hear the news?" Fred asked us. "Noelle McBride is missing."

"What?" Sam said.

"She disappeared. No one's seen her since karaoke. Apparently her parents got home really late last night, and when they looked for her this morning, she was gone. They thought she was at the club all day, but I guess she never showed up there, either. They think something really bad might have happened."

"Oh my God." I didn't exactly like Noelle, to say the least—but I hadn't wanted anything bad to happen to her. Well, nothing too bad.

"We took her home last night—we dropped her off after we left the club. She seemed fine then," Sam said.

"She's probably at one of her million boyfriends' places or something," Colin said.

Fred shook his head. "Her parents are asking around and calling everybody—no one's seen her since last night. Callowe's asking around, too."

"Callowe?" I said. The name sounded familiar, but I couldn't place it.

"The chief of police."

My throat felt dry as I remembered Colin pointing him out at karaoke last night. "Maybe she ran away," I suggested.

"I don't know why she would. The Rose Parade's in three days, and you think she'd really miss being queen? That's all she talked about," Fred said. "Noelle's never missed the parade in her whole life and certainly wouldn't now—being queen was her dream."

"You seem to know a lot about Noelle," I said. "Were you friends?"

"Everyone knows a lot about Noelle," Fred answered. "It's kind of hard not to—the most popular girl in school." He rolled his eyes at the word *popular*. "People just talk about her around here. There's not a lot else to gossip about."

"I wonder if they'll postpone the parade," Colin said.

"I don't know." Fred shrugged. "The whole thing is pretty weird."

I thought about watching Noelle climb the steps to her parents' house last night. When we'd driven off, I'd actually thought that I wouldn't mind never seeing her again.

I can't honestly say I was all that broken up over Noelle's absence. I was too busy thinking about Troy. I could hear his voice before I went to sleep. *Yes, Sophie. I've never met anyone like you. With you . . . everything's different. You make me want to be someone. I know people think I'm not that smart, but you can see the real me. When I finish high school, I'm going to go to Yale for English literature: I'll do my thesis on Jane Austen . . .*

I wore my necklace to work the next day. But no one noticed it at first because everyone was talking about what could've happened to Noelle.

"I think it's your boyfriend who did it," Henry said.

"Who? Did what?"

"Your lifeguard boyfriend. To Noelle." He took a finger and ran it across his neck.

"Oh, please. Troy didn't kill her. And he's not my boyfriend."

"I've never seen him buy so may Cokes and ice creams in a week. Well, you can have fun visiting him in the state pen."

I ignored him and wiped down the soda machine.

Chief Callowe and his brother were at the club that morning, too, interviewing anyone who might know something about Noelle's disappearance. Lacey had been with them earlier, and Troy was off with them in the conference room now. I hadn't gotten a chance to ask him about the necklace yet.

Lacey seemed to be enjoying the notoriety. "Callowe tape-recorded our conversation," she said to Tara as they hovered over their nachos at the counter across from me.

"It's so weird without her here," Tara said.

"It's so quiet," Claire said.

"Maybe you'll be queen for the parade, then," Tara said to Lacey. "You were runner-up."

Lacey smiled. "Maybe I will be." She turned to me and asked for a Coke. Her gaze settled on my neck, and her eyeballs looked like they were about to pop out of her head. "Oh my God." She pointed at me.

"What?" I said.

"You're *wearing* Noelle's *necklace*."

"What are you talking about? This is mine."

She gaped at me. "Where did you get that?"

"I—it was a gift." I fingered it. "From, um, a secret admirer." I realized how ridiculous that sounded as soon as I'd said it.

Lacey gave me a strange look. "That's Noelle's necklace. I know it is."

"Maybe she had a similar one," I said. Would Troy buy the same necklace for Noelle as for me? He might not be a genius, but would he really be *that* stupid? It had to just be a misunderstanding. Maybe Lacey was trying to freak me out. If so, it wasn't going to work. I frothed some milk in the cappuccino machine so loudly that they couldn't even hear each other, and finally they walked away.

At lunchtime Fern asked Sam and me if we wanted to eat with her in her office.

"Have you heard what everyone's talking about? I don't believe it. Of course they say things like that. I hope you don't listen to them, don't think that they're true," Fern said. She had a photo of her grown daughter on the wall and two framed needlepoints: *I LOVE MY POODLE* and *HOME IS WHERE YOUR POODLE IS.*

"What do you mean?" I dipped a french fry into ketchup.

"What they're saying. That you two were the last ones to see Noelle, so maybe you're involved in her disappearance. I think it's just 'cause you're new in town."

"We have no idea what happened to her," Sam said. "We hardly even knew her."

"I know that; it's just what people are saying." Fern fiddled nervously with her straw. "It's a small town, and the McBrides have a lot of power. They've financed half the town, for God's sake. I just want you two to be careful. People can be warm and friendly here—but they can also be extremely judgmental."

"Oh, great," Sam moaned as she walked—and I slowly biked—home from the club that night. The car had been acting up again; Chester was going to take a look at it during the next week. "This is exactly what we wanted to avoid," she said. "I thought Venice was supposed to be a boring, dull old town, where nothing really happened. I can't believe the biggest thing to happen in decades occurs right after we move here."

"She's probably just with some new boyfriend somewhere, like Colin said," I told Sam. "She's probably just . . . I don't know. It's not like anyone in town seems to miss her." I was still more concerned with Troy than with Noelle. He hadn't come back to work after he'd talked to the police. I didn't tell Sam about Lacey pointing to my necklace; it just didn't make sense, so why bring it up? I didn't want to upset her even more than she was already.

We decided we wouldn't worry about the whole Noelle situation for the time being. There wasn't anything we could do about it, anyway. "It'll probably just blow over," I told Sam. "She'll call her parents from wherever she is, and they'll go bring her home and then everyone will forget it even happened." I wasn't exactly looking forward to Noelle's return, but I figured it was inevitable.

We got home, cooked dinner, and watched *Seinfeld* reruns on TV. Right before we went to bed, there was a knock on the door—it was Colin.

"Noelle's car was found," he said. "It's under the bridge just outside of town, half submerged in the water. She wasn't in it, and they haven't found her body."

Seven

As soon as I put on my pink apron the next morning, Chief Callowe and his brother, Officer Alby, appeared at the counter.

"Soda?" I asked hopefully.

"We'd like to speak to you," Callowe said.

My neck prickled. It felt just like the time I was called into the principal's office at my elementary school, PS 11 Queens, for a misfired spitball that had hit the back of my teacher Mr. Feiner's head.

Sam was already waiting in the conference room.

"It's come to our attention that you two were probably the last ones to see Noelle McBride," Callowe said.

"We just dropped her off," Sam said. "She didn't really say much."

"She didn't mention going anywhere? What she was thinking? Plans? Fights, discussions, dissatisfaction?"

"We overheard her having a fight with her boyfriend—um, Troy—earlier that night," Sam said. "But she didn't talk to us about it."

Callowe looked at me. "And you had an argument with Ms. McBride, too."

"She kind of picked on me," I said. "But it wasn't anything serious. It wasn't a big deal."

I thought for a second I was going to hyperventilate. It was as if I had to suppress every cell in my being from screaming, "I'm not Sophia Shattenberg, I'm not a runaway, I'm not Jewish, I swear!" I concentrated on heeding Difriggio's advice and keeping my New York accent in check—to avoid saying *cawfee, cawl, tawk,* et cetera.

"Did you see her go into the house and shut the door?" Callowe asked.

We both nodded.

"We understand that you're wearing a necklace that might have belonged to Ms. McBride," he said to me.

"I don't think so. It was given to me as a gift. I don't know who it's from, though—I found it in my mailbox. I have the note."

I passed it to Callowe.

"We'd like to keep this and the necklace. Evidence," Officer Alby said.

"Evidence? Of what?" Sam asked.

"To see if it's Ms. McBride's and, if so, how you happen to have it."

This was so weird. How had we gotten wrapped up in all this?

"We just wanted to clear a few things up, too. You are Sam and Fiona Scott of Cleveland?" Alby said, reading off a sheet. "Ages twenty-one and fifteen. Sam, you're Fiona's legal guardian."

We both nodded again. I could feel my face reddening but tried to stop it. *Please don't figure us out,* I kept thinking. *Everything will be all right. Everything will be all right.*

Alby wrote down our current address and phone number, and they let us go. Sam and I were both quiet as she walked me out to the pool.

"I thought I was going to have a heart attack in there," I whispered when we were out of earshot. "Do you think we're in trouble?" I could feel tears beginning to well up. "I'm sorry I got us into this mess," I said.

"It's not your fault." Sam put her arm around me, and I leaned into her. "It'll be okay. We haven't done anything wrong. Difriggio said our new IDs are airtight. I'll go see him tomorrow, and see if he knows anything about Callowe, and whether this is really a problem, and what we should do."

She sounded so sensible, while I just wanted to run screaming through the Rose Club grounds. I'd have done anything to just relax into my dad's hug, and smell the sweet laundry-detergent smell of his shirt, and feel safe and protected. I drew my arm more tightly through my sister's.

Sam and I both had the next day, Sunday, off from work. After breakfast she took the bus to see Difriggio. Since we'd been having trouble with the car again, she was afraid it might not make it to Indianapolis and back. Meanwhile, I was supposed to stay at home and do housework and laundry and practice my bike-riding skills. The car was parked in the driveway—Sam was going to drop it off at Chester's on Monday.

I put a load of laundry in the machine and switched on the TV, but nothing good was on. I had the sudden urge to watch a movie—something romantic and old with Audrey Hepburn, like *Roman Holiday* or *How to Steal a Million*. I'd pretend that I was Audrey and Troy was Gregory Peck or Peter O'Toole.

I decided to run to Video Paradise to get something to watch while I folded laundry. The thing was, the video store was four miles away. I thought for a second about coasting there on the bike, but then I'd have to go on a really busy road, which was dangerous. When you looked at the matter objectively, if I drove, then I'd actually have more time to practice my bike-riding skills later in the safety of our block. I tried calling Ethel, but there wasn't a scheduled stop for three hours, and she was getting her hair done, so she couldn't come earlier.

I decided to drive to the video store. I knew Sam would kill me if she found out, but it was such a short drive—just a few minutes—and what could go wrong in that amount of time? It didn't even really seem like driving. In fact, I could probably keep the car in neutral and *coast* the four miles down to the store. It was practically the *same* as biking if you thought about it.

At the video store I ran into Chester, who was renting *The Yearling*.

"What you got there?" he asked me.

"Roman Holiday."

"Why do you need *Roman Holiday* when you've got Venice holiday right here!" He waved out the window.

I mustered a laugh. I wandered over to the freezer case in the front of the store, which sold ice cream. I picked out a pint of double chocolate chip—beside it was a box of Enid's favorite brand of twenty-calorie Fudgsicles. I could barely contain a scream and walked to the checkout counter, where Colin's friend Fred was working the register.

"Old-movie buff, I see," Fred said.

"Yup."

"Double chocolate chip. Yum. Where's your sister?"

"Oh—she's just out." I looked out the window at our car in the parking lot. I didn't want him to notice that I'd driven there, in case he mentioned it to Sam.

I left the store and got back in the car.

Three blocks from home I heard a siren behind me.

It was Officer Alby. I pulled over, trying very hard to breathe normally.

He was finishing up the remains of a powdered-sugar doughnut; white sugar clung to his small mustache. He seemed completely unashamed of living up to the cop-doughnut cliché. "There was a stop sign back there," he said.

"Oh," I said. I knew I'd stopped, but he seemed convinced otherwise.

"Can I see your license?" he asked.

"Um." I pretended to fish around in my pocket for a second. "Actually, I don't have one."

He lowered his eyes. "Does your sister know you're out here?"

I stared at the steering wheel. "I just went to the video store. It was only a few miles."

"Hmm." I saw him fiddle with his notebook, as if he

was looking for guidelines on how to handle this situation. "Uh, just a sec."

He turned on his radio and said, "Hi—brother? It's Junior. I know you're off today, but I've got a, uh, minor here—that girl Fiona?" He said something muffled. "I know it's your only day off. I know you said not to bother you. Yes, I heard you. But she's, uh, *driving without a license.*" He was practically whining; I wondered if I sounded like that when Sam and I argued. He walked farther away from the car so I couldn't hear, and when he came back, he said, "I'm not going to give you a ticket, but I'm going to tell your sister about this."

I couldn't believe it. Sam was going to kill me. I thought for a second about driving off and never returning. Maybe I could finally go to the Bahamas.

"Let me see the registration, please."

I opened the glove compartment. There were about five hundred maps in there. I pulled out the registration to show him, and he copied the information down. Then he looked around the car. I guessed his brother had told him to do that; he didn't seem quite sharp enough to think to do it on his own. He pointed at a dark brown smear on the passenger's seat. "What is that?" he asked.

"Chocolate, I think," I said. "Probably from a doughnut." I thought the mention of a doughnut might appease him. Maybe I could bribe him with a lifetime supply.

"That's not from a doughnut," he said.

What was he, a doughnut detective? "I don't know, maybe it's ink, then," I said. "Or melted lipstick."

He opened the passenger side door and examined

the stain. "I think that's blood," he said. He seemed suddenly very serious; his ears turned nearly as red as his hair. "We're going to have to bring this car to the station."

I sent a silent plea out to my parents. Why was this happening? I used to plead to my mom, wherever she was, when I got a bad grade in school, or a guy I had a crush on didn't like me back, or anything bad happened . . . Now I pleaded to both my parents. If they were watching over us, then I hoped they would help out a little right now.

Officer Alby called another police officer to the scene, gave him the keys to our car to drive it to the station, then took me home in his squad car. I couldn't believe this was happening. My head pounded so loudly, I could hardly think. Why was everything going wrong? If the police didn't arrest me, then Sam would surely have me murdered. I tried desperately to think of something to do.

I wished I could call someone. Wilda? Fern? I didn't want them knowing that I was in trouble. The only person I could think of who I could ask for help was Colin.

Eight

I biked straight from our house to the junk shop. Tears streamed down my face; I just didn't understand why bad things wouldn't stop coming our way and why I kept getting into so much trouble.

"What happened? Sophie—" Colin came up to me, and I sank into his arms before I knew what I was doing.

I cried harder than I had since our dad's funeral. It was as if the floodgates had opened all of a sudden, and all this pent-up sadness and frustration came pouring out.

"Is Sam okay? Did something happen?" Colin asked.

I waited for my sobs to calm down a little and then told him what had happened with Alby. My voice was crackly and my nose kept running; he handed me a box of tissues.

"It'll be okay," he said. He smoothed my hair. It felt so good to be enveloped in his arms. His light brown T-shirt was soft and worn in and smelled like cinnamon. I'd never had a close guy friend before, but there was something about Colin that made him so easy to talk to. His voice was calm and quiet. I think he understood, without my even saying it, that I wasn't just crying over the confrontation with Alby, but over everything else, too. The "car accident" that he thought had killed my parents.

After a while my tears stopped, and he brought me a hot chocolate with mini marshmallows; it was warm outside but cool inside the shop. I blew my nose and slowly filled the wastebasket with a small mountain of crumpled tissues, and began to feel a little better.

"Sometimes I wish I could be more like Sam," I said. "She hardly ever cries."

"Crying's not a bad thing," he said. "She'll probably let it all out, too, sometime."

"Do you ever—do you cry over your mom?"

He sat beside me on the sofa and nodded. "My dad is like Sam—he never cried, not really. He just went off by himself to be alone. Now he just travels all the time. But I cried a lot while she was sick and after she died, and I still cry over it sometimes. I still miss her."

"How did she die?" I asked him.

"She had cancer. Breast cancer."

"Oh. That's really awful."

"It went on for a long time. By the time she died, I guess I was kind of prepared for it, if that's possible. I don't know. I don't know if I could've dealt with it if it had been an accident, like it was for you. And your father, too . . ."

"It's just so weird . . . sometimes I go along and I forget that they're dead. And then I remember, and it's just such a horrible feeling. Like my whole world has disappeared."

He nodded.

I sipped my hot chocolate. There was something soothing about being in Colin's junk shop; I loved being surrounded by all that stuff. I liked thinking about how it had once belonged to other people, that others had loved these things and lost them, and then Colin helped them find new homes.

I rubbed my forehead; I had a huge headache. "I don't want to go back home. Sam's going to murder me when she finds out about this whole police thing. Seriously. She's going to kill me."

"I'm sure it's really not that big a deal," he said. "Alby's usually pretty harmless. He's not the brightest light on the Christmas tree, to say the least. Why would he get so freaked out about a little spot on the car? That doesn't make sense."

"I don't know. I had this weird feeling that he was sort of following me, even, waiting for me to do something wrong, after that whole interrogation about Noelle. I just don't think Chief Callowe and his brother trust us. I got the feeling that they think Sam or I had something to do with Noelle disappearing."

Colin shook his head. "This is a small, weird town you landed in."

I stared at my empty mug. We were quiet for a while, and then I finally mustered up the courage to ask him to help me. "Maybe we can, um, make up a story or something about the car to tell Sam."

"Like what?"

"I could tell her you had to borrow it."

"Why would I borrow it?"

"You had an emergency or something, and Fred had your car—Sam knows Fred only has a bike—so you took ours. Alby said I'd get it back tomorrow, so we can go pick it up and Sam will never know what really happened."

He took a deep breath. "Sophie, I don't know . . ."

"Please. Please . . . she's going to kill me otherwise. She's never going to let me leave the house again. She's going to sulk and yell at me for weeks . . ." I thought of the time I'd borrowed twenty dollars from her and lost it in a taxi. She'd made me repay it with interest, after barely speaking to me for a month. And that was before she was my "legal guardian."

"Please. She's never going to forgive me if she finds out. She's never going to trust me again."

After a while he shook his head. "All right." I could tell that my coming in crying might have had something to do with winning him over.

We came up with a story: Celeste had taken a fall in her house (this had actually happened a couple of times before, Colin said)—she lived a mile away and needed help. He had lent his own car to Fred, so he'd borrowed ours to drive out there. Once at Celeste's, after having helped her, he couldn't get our car started. He'd tell Sam that he'd go out there tomorrow and jump it and drop it off at Chester's for us.

It sounded perfect.

"I can't believe I'm going along with this," he said.

"It's for a good cause," I said. "You're saving my life. And I'll pay you back somehow—I'll help you with the shop, or I'll organize your bookshelves—"

"I'll try and think of something." He grinned.

For a second I almost thought he was flirting with me. I raised my eyebrows at him, and his cheeks flushed.

"Sophie, you don't need to pay me back," he said. "I was kidding."

"Right. Of course," I said.

At home I monitored all the phone calls. Colin had said that the police would probably call to make sure that Sam knew what had happened, and I didn't want her to come home to a message on the machine. Sure enough, the call came in the late afternoon.

"Is this Miss Sam Scott?" a female voice asked.

"Yes, it is." I deepened my voice, trying to sound older, like my sister. At least all those voice modulation techniques we learned at school were finally good for something.

The woman's voice was in such a monotone, she sounded like a radio recording. "I'm calling from the Venice Police Department. A Miss Fiona Scott—you're her legal guardian, right? She was given a warning today about driving without a license. We wanted to make sure you knew."

"Oh, I know," I said. "I've talked to her about it. She won't do it again."

"All right, then, just policy to confirm you're aware of the incident. Have a nice day, ma'am."

Sam returned from Indianapolis a couple of hours later. She threw her bag on the rug and sprawled on the couch with her arm over her eyes.

"Um, are you okay?" I asked. My stomach felt like a colony of jumping beans was partying away inside it. Had she noticed that the car was missing from the driveway?

"Difriggio gave me some news—Enid put our house on the market. There've already been offers," Sam said.

"Offers? We've only been gone three weeks."

"She moves fast. She probably just wants the money."

I slumped into the armchair beside her. "I thought—I thought she'd hold on to it." I felt like a ball of fur had landed in my throat. How could she sell it so quickly? I pictured all the furniture, paintings, books, and tchotchkes we'd left behind . . . I missed it all, and I couldn't believe everything would be gone. For good.

"I wish we could just go back," I said.

"We can't." Her voice was faint and tired.

She stuck out her arms, and I squished in beside her on the couch. "Sopheleh," she said. She'd never called me that before; only my dad had. We sat there together for a long time, without speaking. I felt guilty for not telling her what had happened while she was gone—but it would be worse to admit the truth.

I wondered what our dad would think about the house being sold. He had loved that house so much. He'd been born in Poland, and he and his parents had been the only members of his family to survive the Holocaust. His parents had settled in our neighborhood in Sunnyside, Queens, and the house Sam and I grew up in was just a block away from where our dad had grown up, though his parents died when we were young, so we never really knew them well. Why had he been so blind to Enid? I think, in some ways, he'd never really recovered from our mom's death. He'd thought Enid would make things better and really trusted that she would do her best for us.

I wondered if any of us had really recovered from our mom's death. I wondered if you ever really recovered from losing anyone. Or from losing a place you loved . . . your home. I guess it's one thing to leave a place when you know you'll be able to go back to it. But to leave it and have it disappear without you—it made me feel lost and rootless all the more. *Home.* I'd never even really appreciated having one until it was gone.

"Ugh, I need a Yoo-Hoo," Sam said. "Do we have any?"

I got one out of the fridge. Yoo-Hoo was her ultimate comfort food. When she was sad or depressed, all she wanted was Yoo-Hoo. We always kept a six-pack around for times like these.

She drank it down in about three gulps and got herself another. When she'd finished that, she said, "There's some good news, too, at least. Difriggio says Callowe and Alby aren't much of a threat. Their police station is a laughingstock. He doesn't think we have anything to worry about. That's one of the reasons why he thought Venice was such a great place for us to settle in—because the police here are so incompetent."

I picked the lint off my jeans, praying that was true, and that hopefully Callowe and Alby were competent enough to find out what really happened to Noelle, but not competent enough to figure out who we were. And I hoped Sam would never learn about my run-in with Alby earlier that afternoon.

Nine

Soon after I got to work the next morning, Henry passed the phone to me. "It's for you."

"Hello?" I said.

"The crow flies over the river," a voice whispered slowly.

"What?"

"Uh, it's Colin. That was code."

"Oh." I laughed. "For what?"

"I don't know. But everything went according to plan. I got the car from the station—Chester said it'll be ready Wednesday. You'll hardly even notice the little piece of the passenger seat that's missing where they cut out the stain."

"Good. Thanks—thank you so much." Henry was listening; I didn't want to say anything too revealing. "The porpoise talks underwater," I whispered.

"Is that code?" Colin said.

"Yeah. Code for: My boss needs to stop eavesdropping."

Colin laughed, and Henry made a huffing noise.

My whole body relaxed. Now the only thing to watch out for was the phone call that would come when the test results came back. The blood—if it even *was* blood and not chocolate, as I suspected—was probably from someone who'd had the car ages ago . . . I decided I didn't even need to worry about it.

Anyway, there were more distracting things at the country club. Such as Troy. I hadn't had a chance to ask him about the necklace yet. I kept glancing at him throughout the morning. Finally, during a lag in customers, I decided to go over there.

He was draped across the small white tower, his tanned legs dark against the white paint. Fonzie's leash was tied to the tower, and he was napping in the grass.

"Hi, Troy," I said.

"Hi, Fiona."

"Um, it's Sophie." I patted Fonzie. "I really like your dawg." *Dawg?* Who said that? I coughed and said, *"Dog,"* clearly, trying to stifle my embarrassment. But Troy didn't seem to notice. He leaned back and took a sip from his water bottle. His chest muscles glistened in the sun.

"Um, it was from you, right?" I asked.

He smiled sheepishly. "What are you talking about?"

"The necklace. In my mailbox."

He leaned closer. "Did you like it?"

My face felt warm. I nodded.

"Why aren't you wearing it?"

"Um—because the police took it, actually. They think it's Noelle's."

He blinked. "That's ridiculous."

"Lacey told them it was Noelle's."

"Lacey's mixed up," he said. "She doesn't know what she's talking about. I saw it, and I thought of you. I thought, Fiona would like this necklace. It would look great on her."

I didn't know what to say. I didn't know why sometimes, when I was around certain guys, my brain turned
into melted mozzarella. While we talked, I couldn't stop
thinking about what it would be like to kiss him. I'd only
kissed three guys in my life—two had been skinny, pale,
artsy types from my school, and one had been a peck on
the lips at my friend Aaron Katz's bar mitzvah when I was
twelve, so you couldn't even really count it. The most I'd
ever done was when I'd made out with Randy Chaefsky
on the number 7 train home from school in February. We'd
been in the last car of the train all by ourselves from
Times Square to Queensboro Plaza, and we'd kissed and
I'd let him run his hands up and around my bra.

I was brought out of my reverie by Henry, who trilled
behind us, "Careful, Fiona, you might meet the same
fate as Noelle. A customer's waiting back at the stand."

"What did he say?" Troy asked.

I shook my head. "Ignore him."

"So, what are you doing Friday night?"

"Friday? Um . . ." What did I do every night? Eat.
Read. Sleep. "Nothing."

"I think we should go to the drive-in."

"Sounds like fun," I said, and before I could stop
myself, we'd agreed that he'd pick me up at home on
Friday night.

I walked back to the concessions stand, trying to
hold back a grin. Troy Howard had just asked me out.
Troy Howard, pinnacle of human perfection. Me. Me!
Why me? This was the best thing that had happened to
me, probably *ever*. Oh God, if I could only call Viv and

tell her. I'd had a lot of crushes, but I'd never had a real date before.

What would I wear? And how on earth would I tell Sam?

That night Sam and I made our mom's blueberry blintzes for dinner.

"Stock market's up," Sam said as she prepared the salad. "The Dow jumped seventy-five points today."

"Great! And the weather's been so nice lately, too." I added really quickly: "BythewayI'vegotadatewithTroy-Fridaynight."

"What'd you just say?" She squinted at me.

"I'm going out with Troy?" I said it more to the frying blintzes than to her.

"You're kidding me."

"Well, he asked, and—well—" I shrugged.

"Sophie." She put down her salad tongs. "You're not going out with him. He's bad news. Not only does he have the IQ of a piece of steak, but he's just tacky. I mean, his girlfriend disappeared." Here she squelched my noises of protest. "I don't want to hear from you again that they were broken up, blah blah blah. She's *gone!* He should be out looking for her or be in mourning over her or something. In fact, I *forbid* you to go out with him."

"You can't *forbid* me to go out with him."

"Um, yes, I can. I forbid it. Or else I'm going to tell Difriggio."

"You're going to tell *Difriggio?* And what's he going to do? Sic Cubby on me?"

"No, he'll tell you I'm right. Really, Sophie. It just

looks bad. I mean, *really*. What do you think Mommy and Daddy would have said about Troy?" Here she let out a little laugh.

I'd often asked her what our mom would have thought of guys I had crushes on; it had become a sort of game, almost: "Do you think Mommy would have liked him?" I'd ask, about Randy Chaefsky or Wyatt Kroll, who worked at Rosario's Pizza on Skillman Avenue in Queens. Usually Sam would say, "No," since most of the guys I had crushes on she considered vapid, brainless, or potential drug addicts. I doubted if my dad would really have liked Troy, either—he wasn't exactly the bookish type. Whenever I asked my dad if he liked a certain guy, he'd say dryly, "So long as he can read without moving his lips," from behind his newspaper.

I was pretty sure Troy could do that.

"He's just so cute," I pleaded to Sam. "When in my life will I get to go out with someone so good-looking again? Never. In New York that guy wouldn't look twice at me. There just aren't as many girls here."

"There are plenty of girls; he's just dated all of them already except for you. You know it's not the right thing to do, to go out with him."

I flipped the blintzes, not saying anything.

"Real guys aren't like Troy—they're deeper. They have personalities," she said.

"And how would you know?" I snapped. Sam had never even kissed anyone, ever, as far as I knew.

Her eyes filled with hurt, and I felt a twinge of guilt.

"I'm sorry," I said. "I didn't mean it that way."

She shrugged, her expression returning to its normal, disapproving state. "Anyway, there are more important things in the world than mooning over boys."

We ate our blintzes in silence.

I knew Sam had a point about Troy. It wasn't the greatest timing, with Noelle being gone and everything. But was I supposed to forsake the golden glory of my youth in this tiny town? If things weren't bad enough already, with our parents gone and our whole lives uprooted, I had to deny myself a little romance also?

"Fine, I won't go out with him until the whole Noelle thing is cleared up," I said as I loaded the dishwasher. "But after she comes back or it's discovered that she's run away to Australia—we can only hope—then I'm going out with Troy. And in the meantime we'll need to get cable. I'll have to live vicariously through the characters on TV."

She conceded. "Maybe. I don't know if it can fit in our budget."

"I thought we had three hundred thousand dollars!"

"We do—but we might need it, in case—you never know what might happen."

I sighed, annoyed. Sometimes I wondered if I would've been better off at the Langmoor Academy. At least there I could've found myself a handsome Yukon igloo dweller.

"I'm glad you're putting it off," she said. She began scrubbing pots. "All right. I guess we can get cable."

I grinned.

The next day at work I told Troy that I'd forgotten that we'd already made plans with Wilda and Fern for

Friday night. He took it well—if anything, it seemed to pique his interest in me even more.

"All right, Fiona. You know where to find me." His voice made my knees melt. I wandered back to work, where even Henry couldn't take away the excited whirl in my stomach from looking forward to my date—sometime soon—with Troy.

The next few days passed uneventfully—pouring sodas, gazing at Troy, dinner at the Petal Diner, shopping on-line, pouring sodas, gazing at Troy. At least postponing the date had given me more time to put a new outfit together—I even ordered a new tube top. Then one morning before work—I'd gotten up early that day since the cable man was supposed to come—there was a knock on the door. I opened it, and Alby was standing on our front porch, staring at me with a half-menacing, half-befuddled look.

He told me I had to come down to the station with him.

I was trying to keep the door partly closed, but Sam overheard from the kitchen. "What's going on out there?" she said. She pushed past me and stared at Alby.

"We need you two to come in for questioning."

Sam and I didn't speak to each other as we rode in the back of Alby's squad car. I was so scared, I thought I was going to faint. Visions of women's prisons and gang tattoos and catfights with Sporks ran through my head. My hands were trembling so badly, I finally shoved them under my legs.

Alby brought us into the police station, and Callowe

himself joined us in the "interview" room, which looked like a large closet with a table, chairs, a Rose Parade poster, and a coffeepot. It was nothing like the way it looked on *Law & Order*. I remembered what Difriggio had said, that Callowe and his brother were completely incompetent, and tried to stop being scared.

"The test came back, and the blood we found on the seat of your car is a match for Noelle," Callowe told us.

"What blood?" Sam asked. "What's going on?"

"The blood found on the seat of your Buick."

"That's impossible," I said. "It's a mistake. Or a cover-up! It's—it's a conspiracy!" I knew I sounded like a lunatic, but this whole situation seemed too unbelievable. What did they think, that we'd murdered Noelle and washed all of the blood off the seats but missed a spot?

"Wait a minute," Sam said. "What's going on? What blood?"

"The blood on the seat of your '78 Buick." He ruffled through papers in a file, then removed a form. "A call was made to you informing you of the incident."

Sam's eyebrows drifted up her forehead. "I never got any call."

"It says here Sam Scott was informed via telephone that same day."

"Um—that was me," I said quietly. "I answered the phone."

Callowe let out a huge sigh and took it upon himself to enlighten Sam as to my whereabouts the day Alby pulled me over and my driving without a license, et cetera, and my long list of depraved sins.

Her face turned a shade of red that I'd never before seen on a human being. I wouldn't have been surprised if she'd grabbed Callowe's nightstick and taken a mad swipe at me. For a moment I was actually thankful that I was under the protection of the police.

Callowe and Alby stepped out of the room for a second to confer. When they returned, they said they were going to question us separately. Alby would talk to Sam in the coffee room; Callowe would talk to me in his office.

I sat in a little wooden chair across from his desk, which was covered with stacks of paper and file folders and tchotchkes—little ceramic animals and mouse figurines. I'd never heard of a cop with an entire Hallmark store on his desk before.

"Miss Fiona Scott," he said. "Why didn't you tell your sister about the car?"

"I just didn't want her to be mad," I said weakly.

"I see." He looked down at a paper on his desk. "And what is your explanation for blood matching Noelle's being found on your car seat?"

"Um, I don't know, I thought it was melted chocolate," I murmured.

I glanced around his walls—more Rose Festival posters and a painting of the canal with water in it. I stared at a figurine of a cow playing the bagpipes. I wondered if I should concoct a story like in the movie *The Usual Suspects*.

"I'd like for you to review the events of the night that you drove Noelle home, one more time."

"All she did was get in the car, we drove her home, and

she got out," I said. "I really think this whole blood-being-a-match thing is suspicious. I think we've been set up."

He raised his eyebrows as if actually considering this for a moment and stared at a Rose Festival 2000 poster. Then his expression went suddenly blank. He actually looked . . . well, bored—as if questioning a teenage girl was one of the last things on earth that he wanted to be doing.

"Chief Callowe?" I said.

He shook himself back to the present. "Yes?"

"You need to believe us, that we're telling the truth. We had nothing to do with Noelle disappearing."

He sat back in his chair, and at that moment Alby and Sam appeared in the doorway. "It was a cut," Alby said. "The girl cut her leg."

"Excuse me?" Callowe said.

"Noelle banged her leg on the edge of our car when she was getting into it," Sam explained. "It's kind of jagged and really rusty and she yelped about it—"

"It's a jagged edge," Alby concurred. "That's true. I've seen it myself."

Callowe considered this for a moment.

"I think she's telling the truth," Alby told him.

"It's a possibility, but we don't know what's for certain, Miss Scott," Callowe said. "We're going to keep looking into the case. I think you should stay around here for a while—no plans to leave town anytime soon, I hope?"

We shook our heads.

At home Sam let me have it.

"How could you be such an idiot? I don't understand.

I mean, we're related, aren't we? Supposedly we have the same gene pool. The same brain cells. Though it seems, at the moment, that some of us choose not to use those brain cells much of the time."

I sat there and endured it. I knew I was at fault. "I'm sorry," was all I could think to say.

She didn't accept my apology; she just retreated to the kitchen and banged around in there, putting things away. We went to bed without speaking. It was awful. I couldn't stand having her this angry with me. The truth was that without her, I had no idea what I would do, where I would be. She was all that I had in the world— she was my home.

I lay awake in my bed, staring at the ceiling, and finally after several sleepless hours I creaked open the door to her room, lifted up the quilt quietly, and crawled in beside her like I used to do when we were little.

She groaned and mumbled something unintelligible and went back to sleep. But when I awoke in the morning, she was curled beside me, one arm hugging me close to her chest.

Ten

I stopped by Colin's store before work the next day. "Sam found out," I said.

"I heard. News travels fast here. Alby bought a doughnut at the Petal this morning and told the story to the crowd. So I think everyone knows they took you guys in."

"Oh, great," I said. "Is an angry mob going to come by our house with torches?"

"No time soon, I hope. The town's divided . . . Wilda, Fern, and Chester all defend you, but Bea, from the Rose Society—which is largely funded by the McBrides, by the way—is asking questions. She thinks the blood match is suspicious. I know, it's completely ridiculous. It's just they don't really know you; that's the problem. Also, people in town are grumpy that the Rose Parade's been postponed till Noelle turns up."

"Do people really think we did something to her?"

He shrugged. "I don't know. Not to freak you out, but rumor has it the McBrides hired a private investigator to look into you, too."

"You're kidding."

"It's just a rumor; I don't know if it's true. Fred heard it from someone at the video store who heard it from someone else."

He pulled out something from behind the register. "Here—I found this in some boxes of books I was sorting through, and I thought you'd like it."

It was an old, hardcover edition of Anne Frank's *Diary of a Young Girl.*

My fingers quivered when he handed it to me. Did he suspect that we were Jewish? That we were on the run? Had I said *"tchotchke"* and *"dawg"* and *"cawfee"* too many times in front of him? Had he seen that box of matzo meal that I'd bought even though Sam had told me not to? (The matzo meal had taken some hunting for in the Kroger's—I found it in the "ethnic foods" section, between the salsa and soy sauce.)

"Why'd you want to give me this . . . ?" I asked him.

"I just thought you'd like it." He shrugged. "Have you read it before?"

"No," I lied. Maybe I was just being paranoid.

In truth, the diary was one of my favorite books—I'd read it five years ago, and it had changed my life in the way that great books did. Sometimes I'd be going along in the midst of some misery and think, *How would Anne Frank handle this? Or Scout Finch from* To Kill a Mockingbird? *Or Anne of Green Gables?* They were all so strong and seemed capable of overcoming anything. Just thinking of them made me feel less alone.

"It's a rare edition. I just thought you might like to have it."

"Thanks," I said quietly.

I didn't have to be at work for almost an hour, so I sat in one of the comfy chairs in his shop and leafed through the book. I opened to a page where she'd written, *The best remedy for those who are afraid, lonely, or unhappy is to go outside . . .* As long as there's nature, she wrote, *there will always be comfort for every sorrow, whatever the circumstances may be.*

I thanked Colin again, and Anne's words stayed in my head as I biked to work. I was getting so much better at biking; I even stopped riding the brake constantly as I coasted down hills. I pedaled freely past the cornfields and meadows, the wind breezing by. We were lucky, in so many ways, Sam and I. There was a part of me—a huge part—that was still sick with grief. But I couldn't take for granted that we were free—to go outside and breathe fresh air and live here by ourselves in our pretty house. I was suddenly, for the first time in a long while, grateful for what we had.

I read more of the diary intermittently at work, jumping around through different parts of it, in between customers and on my breaks. Anne wrote about herself: *I have lots of courage, I always feel so strong and as if I can bear a great deal . . . I don't think I shall easily bow down before the blows that inevitably come to everyone.*

I hoped that I could be that strong, that I wouldn't bow down easily, either. I knew I'd already come through a lot. Our mom—who I'd loved more than anyone in the world besides Sam—had been gone for so long. Her disappearance and all the events surrounding her death had been worse than anything I could have ever imagined. And then our father—who had held on for so long—he was gone, too. I still couldn't believe it had happened. Yet here Sam and I were. We'd turned out okay. We weren't even unhappy, really. We were sad about everything we'd lost, but there were moments now—and they were coming more and more frequently—when we laughed so hard and so long that we almost forgot all the miseries we'd endured.

Like last week, at Colin's place. We'd taught him how to play Lorna Scrabble—a version of Scrabble our mom had invented. The rule was that you could use only made-up words, as long as you convincingly announced a plausible definition for them. There was no score, and the only way you could lose was by putting down a real word.

We'd played that game until the late hours of the night, sitting in Colin's shop, long after it was closed.

"Fugtroe," I'd said, arranging my letters on the board as I stared at a rusty metal thing in the corner. "An antique piece of farm equipment."

"Icnatus," Sam put down. "The constellation directly east of Orion."

"Sckwyd," Colin said, feigning a British accent. "An uncommon but very friendly Welsh goblin."

We'd laughed till our stomachs ached, and afterward Sam and I had walked home under the dark, starry sky. I couldn't even remember the last time I'd laughed that hard. I was beginning to feel—even if just a tiny little bit—like my old self again.

Despite letting me sleep in her bed the night before, Sam seemed chilly and distant to me when we came home from work that night. I knew better than to

bother her when she was like this; I gave her her space.
I made baked ziti, and she read Morningstar mutual-
fund reports while she ate. I took my dinner into the living room and watched TV.

When I'd finished the ziti and moved on to chocolate pudding, I heard a strange noise outside. Bushes
rustling. The wind? Then a loud clanking.

I interrupted Sam in the kitchen. "Did you hear that?"

"What?" She put her newsletter down.

"I heard a noise. Outside."

"I didn't hear anything." A minute later a huge
crashing sound roared from behind the house.

She grabbed the long wood back scratcher I'd
bought for her at a rest stop in Ohio, and we crept outside to see what was happening. She poised the back
scratcher like a baseball bat.

"Ooooof," someone groaned from behind our house.

Sprawled between our overturned garbage cans,
my discarded set of broken Conair Big Curls hot rollers,
and a mound of moldy macaroni and cheese lay a rum-
pled, vaguely homeless-looking man. A pickle pro-
truded from his hair.

We crept closer. It was Gus, from the diner.

He stared down at his knee, then flinched.

"What are you doing here?" Sam asked.

He stood with a bit of effort, then limped forward
and stuck out his hand.

"I don't think we've ever met, officially. I'm Gus
Jenkins. Pleased to meet you."

*　　*　　*

We took him inside and gave him an ice pack for his knee. I moistened a paper towel and wiped a huge wad of mayo off his ear.

"What were you doing, looking through our garbage? Are you hungry or something?" Sam held a Band-Aid in midair.

He sighed. "I'm a private investigator. The McBrides hired me to find their daughter."

"Oh." Sam backed away. I could see she was regretting having invited him in.

"You can come back over—I don't bite," he told her.

"You could've just knocked on the door," Sam said. "Instead of poking through our garbage."

He shrugged. He had several days' worth of stubble on his cheeks and wore an old brown suit that was a size too small for him. He seemed about as threatening as a field mouse. Still, Sam's voice was tight—a private investigator poking into our lives was yet another worry, on top of everything else. Even if he seemed kind of schlumpy, to say the least.

"You girls live here by yourselves?"

We nodded.

"You know, you should be a little more careful—two girls on your own, you hear a noise outside, you call the police; you don't go after the culprit with a back scratcher."

"That's nice advice coming from you, the culprit," Sam said, raising her eyebrows.

"And you should keep your curtains closed at night, too. You"—he pointed a finger at me and gave me a paternal look—"you hanging out here in that men's underwear with the curtains wide open! Didn't your parents teach you anything?"

I looked at Sam and rolled my eyes. Who on earth was this guy?

His eyes darted around the kitchen, eyeing our posters. "Cleveland Symphony?" he said.

"Our parents were musicians," Sam said.

We sat there, looking at each other. I used to help my father with his insurance claim investigations; he retired a couple of years after our mom disappeared, but when he was still working, we had some adventures together. Once I had to pretend to be selling Girl Scout cookies to find out if a certain person actually lived at an address, and another time my dad and I sat in his company's surveillance van for six hours until we caught a supposedly housebound man walking around the block. But I'd never gone through anyone's garbage or sat in a stranger's kitchen with mayo in my ear.

"So what were you looking for, exactly, in our garbage?" Sam asked him. "Noelle's body?"

"Very funny."

"The McBrides really hired *you*?" I asked.

"Yes. As a matter of fact, they did." He picked a limp leaf of lettuce off his lapel. "Don't look so surprised." He surveyed the room more closely—the purple curtains and bright furniture. "Feminine touch. Guess it suits some people."

It made me a little nervous, watching him look so closely around the room. Had we left out anything too revealing? I looked around—no, thank God. No matzo meal on the counter for all to see. I made a mental note to put it in an unmarked container and destroy the box in case Gus decided to search our trash again.

"So, have you been an investigator very long?" I asked.

"I was a detective on the force in Indy and Chicago. I just started taking private cases, uh, recently. Speaking of which, since I'm here already, there are a couple of things I'd like to ask you." His eyes settled on the pan of leftover baked ziti on the counter. "By the way, are you eating that?"

"You want some?" I asked.

"Only if you have extra."

I sighed and put some on a plate for him. Maybe this would butter him up a little.

"What questions?" Sam asked, an edge in her voice.

"Let's see. I know your story, from Wilda. About your parents." He lowered his eyes. "Really sorry to hear about that. But I'd like to know what you were up to the night Noelle disappeared."

We'd been through this so many times. We told him the whole story. "We had nothing to do with it," I said, for what felt like the hundredth time.

"I don't even know why people are suspicious of us," Sam said. "We hardly even knew Noelle. You should be questioning Troy—Noelle's *supposed* boyfriend—or Lacey, her *supposed* best friend. Why aren't you poking through *their* garbage?"

"I will," he said. "Just haven't gotten to it yet. Plus you have the best pasta," he said with his mouth full.

When he finished his plate of food—in about three

bites—Sam stretched her arms and yawned. "I'm getting tired," she said. "Think we better get to bed."

"Subtle hint," Gus said. He tried to bend his knee but couldn't; he shouted several expletives. "Oh, sorry," he said. "Forgot I was around two young ladies."

Slowly and painfully he managed to stand up and limp toward the door. "I'll be seeing you," he said.

"Can't wait," Sam said dryly.

We shut the door and watched him limp down the porch steps and around the corner.

"Great," Sam said when he was out of sight. "Just what we needed."

"Seems like he's not exactly the most effective investigator, though." I shrugged.

"I'm going to call Difriggio and see if he has any dirt on him," she said.

"Or mayo on him," I said.

She left a quick message for Difriggio; we sat down at the kitchen table, and I made a pot of tea.

"I know you think I'm featherbrained and everything, but just listen to me for a second. I think that maybe we should investigate this whole Noelle thing ourselves," I said.

She looked at me.

Maybe it was reading the Anne Frank book that was giving me some extra courage, but I felt like we had to do something. We knew a little about investigating from what we'd learned from our dad and the search for our mom. Why wait for the blame to be placed on us (or me, more particularly) when we could clear our names ourselves?

"You just want to find her so you can go out with Troy," she said with a grin. But I could tell she was joking.

"I just want to not go to prison," I said. "Where would I plug in my hair dryer?"

"Good point."

After a minute she said, "I think you're right. Maybe you're not so featherbrained after all."

"Gee, thanks."

She stared at a fleck of sauce on the table. "It's what Daddy would say to do, too—to look for Noelle ourselves. I don't know why I didn't think of it myself."

Difriggio called back that night. After Sam got off the phone, she turned to me with her eyebrows raised.

"Do you remember when Difriggio said he had a contact in Venice? Well, guess who his contact is? Gus Jenkins, private investigator. Gus was on the Indianapolis police force with Difriggio's father."

"Why didn't Difriggio tell us sooner?" I asked.

"Apparently Gus is going through some hard times. I guess finding him sprawled out in our garbage is not exactly uncharacteristic of his investigating skills lately. But he's the only PI in town. Interestingly enough, he used to be the smartest guy on the force—next to Difriggio's dad, that is."

"What happened?"

She shrugged. "Personal stuff, according to Difriggio. Didn't Wilda say his wife left him?"

I nodded. I felt a little sorry for Gus and thought of him sitting in our kitchen earlier that night, looking so disheveled. "So should we be worried about him poking into our backgrounds or what?"

"Well, according to Difriggio we should be careful around everybody. But he said he called Gus not long after we moved here and told Gus that he'd known our parents and asked Gus to look out for us. Gus agreed he would. Difriggio's sense is that despite being hired by the McBrides, Gus is really on our side. Though we still can't take chances, no matter what."

I pressed my lips together, then nodded again. I usually tried my best to forget about the danger we were still in—always in—with Enid after us. The idea of Sam and me alone in our house with only my stuffed polar bear, Ed, to protect us wasn't much of a comfort.

Eleven

We decided to enlist Colin to help in our investigation. He knew more about Noelle and the people around town than we did, and there was no question that he was on our side.

We rang the bell of his shop that evening.

"Time for a game of Lorna Scrabble?" he asked.

"Actually, we've got something else we wanted to talk to you about," Sam said.

We sat down on his comfy sofa and explained what we wanted to do, and then together we made up a list of suspects in the Case of the Disappearing Annoying Popular Girl. (That was what I wrote in my notebook.)

"What did you just write in there?" Colin asked, glancing over my shoulder.

"I thought the case should have a name," I said. "You know. Like *'The Clue in the Diary'*? *'The Secret of the Old Clock'*?"

"Okay, Nancy Drew and Bess," Colin said. "The Case of the Disappearing Annoying Popular Girl. Where should we start?"

"I'm not Bess. She was such a wuss. I'd rather be George," Sam said.

"Fine, *George.*"

We brainstormed everyone we knew who might have had something to do with Noelle's disappearance, or who might have information that could help us solve the case.

> Troy Howard
> Noelle's parents
> Lacey Lanning
> Tara Cody
> Claire Salton
> Greg Burnville (Noelle's ex)

"The thing is, we can't just go up to these people and pepper them with questions. We have to be subtle, or it'll just cast more suspicion on us," Sam said.

We sat there for a few minutes, thinking about it. I doodled in my notebook, drawing waves around Troy's name. Sam glanced at the page and frowned, then almost immediately brightened. "I've got an idea," she blurted. "It's one that Sophie will certainly love."

"What? Does it involve shopping?" Visions of special detective outfits requiring the purchase of minidresses and platform shoes danced through my head.

"No, actually, it involves going on a date with Troy."

This was even better.

"What?" Colin said.

"It's a perfect situation." Sam reached for my notebook. "We'll come up with a list of questions, and you can ask them on the date! He'll have his guard down and he'll never suspect anything, so you can find out everything he knows about Noelle and if he had anything to do with her disappearing."

"I don't think that's a good idea," Colin said. "I mean, what if Troy did have something to do with her disappearance? What if he *killed* her? It's not safe for Sophie to go out with him." His face grew redder with every word. Why did it matter to him so much?

"It's hard enough for Troy to figure out how to tie his shoes in the morning," Sam interrupted. "I seriously doubt the guy is capable of murdering his girlfriend without leaving a trace. I don't think Sophie will be in danger."

"Ex-girlfriend," I corrected.

"Ex-girlfriend," she said. "Anyway, I think you should go out with him this weekend."

I nodded. "Sounds like a good plan." I already had my outfit pictured. My denim miniskirt and my new black tube top, which had just arrived in the mail. Maybe I'd convince Sam to buy me some new jewelry since she seemed in such good spirits.

"I don't know," Colin said. "I don't like this idea."

Sam ignored him completely. "We're gonna aim for Friday night." She handed me back the notebook, then started dictating the questions I was going to ask Troy.

Did you in fact murder Noelle McBride?

"Sophie—I was kidding," Sam said.
"Oh." I crossed it out.

What do you think happened to Noelle?
What was your last conversation with Noelle about?
Did you break up with her? Why?
Did Noelle mention leaving town for any reason?
What have you told the police?
What did you do after leaving karaoke?

The list went on and on. "I'm not going to get a word in edgewise after all these questions," I said. "It's not going to be much of a date."

Sam's tone darkened. "It's not *supposed* to be much of a date. You're only doing this to find out information."

Colin shook his head. "There must be some way to get information from Troy without having to leave Sophie alone with a womanizing meathead."

I wanted to leap in and defend Troy, but I didn't want them to think I was really thinking of it as a date.

"Well, do you have a better idea?" Sam asked him.

He shrugged.

"No? Okay, then. The date it is. Anyway, she'll be in a public place, and I'll give her the cell phone so she can call if she's uncomfortable at all."

I twirled my pen around, trying to hold back a giant grin. Being a detective rocked.

The next morning I went up to Troy at the club and told him I could go out with him after all. I said that I hoped he was still free—and he was.

When Friday night finally came, Troy picked me up in his gray Ford pickup. It had two bumper stickers on the back: IF GOD IS WITHIN, I HOPE HE LIKES ENCHILADAS and I'M NOT AS DUMB AS YOU LOOK.

"Nice truck," I said.

"Thanks." He grinned. When he'd appeared at our doorway, Sam and Colin had been waiting inside, like parents. I was afraid Colin was going to grill Troy on what his plans were for us tonight, but he just stood there, tight-lipped, and told us not to stay out too late.

Of course the whole thing would've been a lot more enjoyable if I hadn't had a novel-length list of questions in my purse.

We were on our way to a restaurant called the Slow Down Hoe Down for dinner and then to the drive-in. I'd decided to wear my black eyelet cardigan over my black tube top and black open-toed heels. I'd painted my toenails pink and even painted in flowers in the middle of my big toenails (an artistic technique that Viv and I had perfected together). Sam hadn't thought it necessary to buy me any new jewelry, but she did chip in for the nail polish.

"You look really beautiful, Fiona," Troy said.

"Thanks." Maybe Fiona wasn't such a bad name after all.

"You know what I like about you? There's something worldly about you. I guess 'cause you're from Cleveland."

"Hmm," I said.

"A woman of the world," he said. "And you smell so good, too. Is that French perfume?"

"No . . ." I was wearing vanilla oil from The Body Shop.

"You smell like a doughnut. Yum," he said.

Doughnut? That wasn't exactly what I'd been going for. Although maybe it explained why Alby had been bugging me so much. "Your truck smells nice, too," I said lamely. Ugh, it must have been so obvious that this was my first real date. I had no idea what I was doing. How embarrassing.

"I call it 'Eau de Fonzie,'" Troy said.

I laughed.

"So how are you liking Venice?" he asked.

"Well, the people seem really nice, for the most part. Except for . . . um, some of them."

"You probably mean my ex-girlfriend. Yep, she was a trip."

I made a mental note of the word choice *was*. Sam might be interested in that. His comment was the perfect entry into the first question on the list:

"What do you think happened to her?" I asked him. Whew—check that one off.

He shrugged. "I dunno."

"I mean, do you think . . . someone did something to her?"

He gripped the steering wheel. "I have no idea."

"Did you talk to her before she left?"

"Nope."

"But that night before—we heard you arguing. After karaoke."

"Are we going to talk about Noelle all night? I'd rather talk about you." His hand brushed my cheek.

Something in me warmed up. Oh, why couldn't I

just go on a date with this supremely handsome hunk of manliness instead of drilling him with questions like Chief Callowe?

We finally arrived at the restaurant. Its walls were covered with stuffed deer and buffalo heads. A huge mechanical bull sat in the middle of the room, with a big brown cowboy hat on its head.

"I love this place. Slow Down Hoe Down!" Troy shouted like a cowboy. "It rhymes."

I cringed. That degree in English literature wasn't seeming too likely.

We sat at a corner table, and a blond hostess gave us menus. She wore shorts so microscopic, she made me feel like I was dressed like an Amish girl. I thought I saw her wink at Troy, too, though maybe I imagined it.

I read the menu. Fried chicken, fried fish, hush puppies, french fries, fried steak. Fried, fried, fried. Not a lot of varied cooking techniques in use.

The waiter came over, and Troy slapped his palm; obviously they knew each other. "Steve-o, can you get us two Buds, *por favor?*"

Ooh, beer. Sam would not be happy. I grinned.

Troy gave me a smoldering look and picked my hand up in his. He ran his fingers over my palm. "Your hands are so small," he said. He measured our palms together and clasped his fingers over mine. Chills traveled through my body and settled in my stomach.

I tried hard to remember the slip of paper folded up in my purse.

"Working at the pool has been a lot nicer since I've

had you to look at, Fiona, over there in your pink apron."

"Really?" I'd never been with a guy who so honestly admitted that he liked me. The most Randy Chaefsky had ever complimented me was the one time he'd said, "Nice skirt, Shattenberg."

"It's fun working there. It's nice looking at you, too, across the pool," I said.

"Acrawss," he said. "You've got such a cute way of talking." He brushed my hair away from my face.

My whole body felt in the clouds. I didn't even care about my accent anymore.

"I'm glad we got this chance to spend time alone together. I've been wanting to get to know you for a long time."

Was he really saying these things? To me?

"Me, too," I said.

Just then the cell phone rang. Sam usually had custody of the phone Felix had given to us—I almost never carried it with me. I was surprised to hear it ring.

"Sorry," I told Troy, and answered it.

"Colin made me call," Sam's voice squeaked. "We wanted to make sure you're okay."

"I'm *fine.*"

"Did you ask him the questions yet?"

"Sam—yeah," I said through my teeth, annoyed.

"Okay, okay, we'll leave you alone. Remember— you're on a work date. This isn't a date date."

"I *know.*" We said good-bye, and I hung up.

"Sorry," I told Troy again. "My sister."

Our beers arrived; I took a long swig. I knew I had to ask

some more of the questions, just to get them over with. "Um, Troy, did you and Noelle really break up before she disappeared? It would just make me feel better if I knew."

"Fiona, you need to stop worrying about her. We're completely over. She never meant anything to me."

"But do you remember that night, after karaoke? Where'd you go?"

"I don't know. Drove around. Didn't really do anything, I guess."

I made a mental note: *No alibi.*

I took another long swig of my beer. Maybe the beer would make me relax. Wasn't that what beer was supposed to do? We placed our order—I ended up going with the fried fish—and I let the conversation move on. We talked about movies, magazines (he only liked to read ones about cars), books (he said, "Why should I read a book when I can see the movie?"), college (he saw no point in going—high school was torture enough), and how he wanted to take me corn detasseling next week.

"Corn what?"

"Detasseling. You never heard of it?" Our food arrived, and as he spoke, he tore into his fried chicken. "Oh, I forgot, you're from Cleveland. Detasseling's all about corn sex. You see, two rows of male corn are planted between six rows of female corn—you have to remove the tassels from the girl plants so they can be fertilized by the boy plants. A machine comes along to chop off most of them, but some get left, and it's up to us to walk down the rows and remove the rest so the corn can, you know, do it."

Had he actually just used the phrase *do it* in relation to

corn? Sam had been right about one thing—a brainiac he was not. My head began to swirl. Not just from the conversation, but from the beer. I tried to focus. After he finished eating, Troy excused himself to the bathroom; while he was gone, I quickly read through my questions and tried to think of how to smoothly get the rest of them answered.

When he returned, I said, "I was wondering, about Noelle—"

"Fiona, I don't want to hear anything more about Noelle."

"It's just, I was kind of curious—"

"I told you, I don't want to talk about her." He actually raised his voice, and anger flashed from his eyes. It was a little frightening, his sudden rage; I clutched my purse to my lap. "You want to know about Noelle?" he snapped. "Well, she was a bitch, and nobody in this town liked her. Everyone's glad she's gone. I'm glad she dumped me."

"She . . . dumped you?"

"Yeah, she did. She was evil. Lying and mean and evil, and she got what she deserved."

I leaned back away from him. It scared me, to hear him talk like this. Maybe Colin was right—maybe Troy had done something to her. I'd been so blinded by his looks, I'd never really thought he could harm someone. But maybe he had. For the first time I doubted my belief that he was innocent.

"Do you know, I don't feel so well," I said. "I don't think I'm really up for the drive-in. I just feel kind of . . . sick."

"I didn't mean to upset you. I'm really sorry. Come on, let's go to the movie."

"I'd just like to go home. Really. I'm not feeling well. I have a . . . stomachache. I'll just get a cab. Or, um, call Ethel, I mean."

"Ethel's not going to come all the way out here. Plus it's nine o'clock. By now she's tucked in bed with rollers in her hair. Come on. The movie'll make you feel better."

"Please. I really need to go home."

I clutched my house keys in my palm the whole ride, ready to impale him with a sharp one if necessary. I didn't know if he was guilty or not, but something in me had changed. He wasn't the Troy Howard I'd thought he was. He suddenly didn't even seem as good-looking—his hair had so much gel in it, it looked kind of greasy. I sat close to the car door in case I had to make a quick getaway. Finally we reached our house.

"Fiona, this didn't go exactly the way I'd planned. I really wanted to have a nice time with you. I think you're real special. And just so cute. It would mean a lot to me if you'd give me another chance."

"Maybe . . . um, thanks for dinner." I was relieved to have made it home safely, though Sam would be mad that I hadn't gotten through all the questions.

He leaned toward me and tried to kiss me on the lips, but all I could think about was that he could very possibly be a murderer. I moved so the kiss landed on my cheek. "Bye!" I said. I ran into the house.

Colin and Sam were waiting for me in the doorway.

"How did it go?" my sister asked. "Did you get answers to all of the questions?"

"Ugh." I slumped down on the table and buried my head in my hands. "That was creepy."

"Did he try something?" There was an angry edge to Colin's voice that I'd never heard before.

"No . . . no. He just kind of freaked out. I kept bringing up Noelle, and he didn't want to talk about it, and then at one point he got really mad. It was a little scary. I got the feeling that maybe he could've actually done something sort of violent."

"I knew it," Colin said to Sam. "We shouldn't have let her go out with him all by herself. Something could've happened." He shook his head.

"Do you really think he did something to her?" Sam asked me.

I shrugged. "I don't know. It's possible. He got a little spooky, talking about Noelle. It was weird." I felt a shiver, thinking of how quickly his personality had changed.

"I think we should follow him," Sam said. "Trail him around for a little while. See what he does."

"You're really getting into this detective thing whole hog," I said. Had I really just used the words *whole hog?* We'd clearly been in the Midwest a little too long.

"I don't know if it's worth it," Colin said, glancing at the clock. It was almost ten. "He's probably just at home with his girlie magazines. What do you think we'll find? Him burying parts of Noelle's body in the woods?"

"Colin," I said. "Gross."

"Sorry."

"No, really. We might find out something," Sam said.

"I think we should do it." She must have been thinking about our dad's investigations—surveillance was his favorite method.

She finally convinced us. We decided to take Colin's van, since our Buick still growled and clanked (even after being repaired and relubed by Chester) and therefore was not a very good choice for surreptitious stalking. We changed into black T-shirts and sweatpants, too; I even tied up my hair with a black scarf. Then we ventured into the night, ready for the surveillance of our first suspect.

Twelve

We climbed into Colin's red Dodge minivan, the back of which was filled with junk that he'd bought at a flea market. "Where should we try first?" he asked.

"I guess Troy's house," Sam said. "Where else do you think he'd go? The arcade? Video store? Strip bar?"

"Brothel?" Colin said.

"Guys," I said, "he's probably just home watching TV."

We embarked on our hunt for Troy. We went by his house (Colin knew where he lived), but his truck wasn't parked outside. We drove by the video store with no luck, and finally Sam suggested that maybe he'd gone to the drive-in without me.

"By himself?" I said.

"Who knows," she said. "It's worth a try."

We drove out there and slowly circled the lots at the three different screens. People had set out beach chairs and coolers in front of their cars, with their radios cranked high, playing the sound of the film.

"Is that it?" Colin said.

We parked a few cars away from a gray Ford pickup. Sam stuck her head out the window, but she couldn't see Troy—a huge SUV was blocking our view.

"Do you see a bumper sticker that says, 'If God Is Within, I Hope He Likes Enchiladas'?" I asked.

Sam opened her door to get a better look. "I can't see the bumper. But I think that's him in there."

"That's so sad, that he went by himself." I suddenly felt a little bad about the whole night. He probably hadn't killed Noelle. Maybe he'd only overreacted to my questions about Noelle because she made him as mad as she'd made me. Maybe I could've been with him right now, sharing an amazing kiss . . .

Sam got out of the car and stepped closer to Troy's truck, then came back and stuck her head in our window. "I don't think he's by himself. There's some blond girl in there with him."

"What?" I said.

We skulked over to Troy's truck. He definitely wasn't by himself. He had his lips all over some chick in really tiny denim shorts. It took me a second, and then I placed her—the hostess from the Slow Down Hoe Down.

"What are you *doing?!*" Before I could stop myself, I'd knocked on the window and was screaming at him.

He opened the door. "Fiona? What—why are you dressed like a bank robber? What are you doing here?"

"This is nice," I said. "Really nice. You were on a date with me two hours ago! Did that mean nothing to you?"

"Well—" His eyebrows raised helplessly.

"You're a pig!" I slammed the door and stormed back toward our car.

"Wow," Sam said. "That was subtle."

"I can't believe him," I muttered. "I mean . . . what

a sleazeball." I kept shaking my head. Thank God I hadn't kissed him.

Sam turned around in her seat and looked at me. "I'm sorry, Soph."

"Yeah." I sighed. So much for my love life. Back to watching others have fun on TV. I'd probably die without ever having a real, normal date, without having to interrogate the person.

We left the drive-in and headed back home.

"Pretty interesting," Colin said. "Maybe Noelle found out about Troy cheating, confronted him, and it turned ugly."

"Ugly enough that Troy killed her?" Sam asked.

Colin shrugged. "You never know."

The next day at the club Sam decided that we should take the Troy matter one step further and confront him with a more professional interrogation.

"Let's just move on to the next suspect. I mean— I've had enough of him," I said.

"But he's still a suspect. We'll just ask him some questions, see if he really has no alibi, and then make sense of the information."

It was worthless to try and reason with her. She waltzed right up to him at his lifeguard station. "Troy. Conference room. One o'clock. We need to talk."

"What—?"

"Be there." She marched off.

Sam was beginning to take this detective thing a little too seriously. Before our lunch break she took the lamp from her office into the conference room and set it up so that it would shine directly into Troy's eyes.

"Listen, Detective Briscoe, this isn't *Law & Order*," I told her. "He doesn't have to talk to us if he doesn't want to."

She ignored me and continued to adjust the lamp. I wasn't sure if I should go along with this, but I didn't have much of a choice. When Sam meant business, you couldn't stop her.

Troy arrived at the conference room exactly on time. I half smiled at him; I was still a little embarrassed about the night before. Plus he was wearing a navy-blue T-shirt that made him look so . . . good. I gulped and then remembered how scary he'd seemed, talking about Noelle. "Sit," Sam told him. She adjusted the lamp so it glared toward him even more brightly. He squinted.

"We just need to get a few facts straight. For the record. On the night that Noelle disappeared, you had a fight with her at the country club, did you not?"

"Um. I did," he said, shifting position.

"And Noelle in fact broke off the relationship with you because you were cheating?"

He nodded solemnly.

"And later that night, after the karaoke and the breakup with Noelle, you were with another girl?"

He looked surprised. "How did you—?"

"The girl from the drive-in last night, I assume. The restaurant girl," Sam said.

"I . . . uh . . ." He finally just nodded. I was impressed with Sam's powers of deduction. Maybe all those Sherlock Holmes stories our dad used to read to us were finally paying off.

"And the necklace was in fact a gift that you had previously given to Noelle, before you regifted it to Sophie."

"What?" I said. "Is that true?"

"Well—Noelle threw it back at me after our fight. It was a great necklace . . . I wanted Fiona to have it."

What a cad. I scowled at him.

"That's charming," Sam said. "Thanks so much for answering our questions." She flicked off the light and started writing down notes. "You're excused," she told him. He scurried out the door.

"How did you figure out he was with that girl after the karaoke? And the necklace?"

"He seemed a little too familiar with that hostess last night . . . I had the feeling that wasn't their first time together, to say the least. And I asked Lacey when she last saw Noelle wearing that necklace—she said the night of karaoke. Then when you said Noelle had broken up with him that night, it made sense that she would've given the necklace back to him. He, in turn, gave it to you."

"I guess I really pick the good ones."

"Aren't you glad you didn't go out with him on a real date?"

I nodded. "I guess so." Still, it was a little hard to let go of my Troy crush. What could possibly make my job interesting now? Certainly not Henry.

"One suspect down, five more to go," Sam said.

*   *   *

That afternoon at work Sam called the McBrides to see if they'd talk to us, but Mrs. McBride hung up on her without further ado. We'd have to figure out some other way to get more information about them; in the meantime we moved on to the other four people on our list—three, really, considering Tara and Claire were basically the same person, conjoined at the hip. We decided we'd try Lacey first. This was easy since she was always poolside at the club—we'd certainly have no trouble finding her.

I took my afternoon break while Lacey was sitting by herself as Tara and Claire flailed away in the pool. I brought Lacey a Diet Coke, and Sam and I sat on the lounge chairs beside her. "We're trying to figure out for ourselves what happened to Noelle," Sam told her. "Since apparently some members of the town think we might have had something to do with it, we're trying to clear our names. We were wondering if we could ask you a couple of things about her."

"Sure," Lacey said. "Why not?" She put down the pad of pink paper she'd been writing on. She seemed in a particularly good mood, and we soon found out why.

"I'm working on my speech for the Rose Parade. If Noelle doesn't come back, I'm going to be queen. I was the runner-up in the contest, you know."

"I didn't know that," Sam said.

"Actually, I deserved to win all along."

"Why?" I asked.

"Well, there's a bunch of criteria you need to meet to get to be queen. You can't be just anyone. You need a 3.4 GPA or higher to make the cut—I've got a 3.7. Noelle only had a 3.1, by the way. Then there are the photos you need to submit of yourself in your Rose Queen dress—I designed my own, and my mom helped sew it. And then—and this is most important—there's your essay."

"Wait a minute—if Noelle only had a 3.1, then how did she win?"

Lacey arched an eyebrow. "That's something I'd like to know, too. But back to my essay. I wrote that as Rose Queen, *I'm* going to save the canal once and for all. You know those things that you put in the bathtub over the drain to stop the water from draining out? Well, my plan is to line the whole bottom of the canal with little plastic things like that so we can hold the rainwater in and it will fill up again. . . ."

"Oh," Sam said. We exchanged looks. *Do not laugh,* I told myself. "Interesting plan," Sam continued. "You definitely should have won."

"So why do you think Noelle won?" I asked.

Lacey looked around us to see if anyone was listening, then lowered her voice. "Honestly, I think something funny was going on. Noelle wanted it so badly, and there's no way she could've won legitimately. It's just not possible."

"Why?" I asked.

"First off, there were her grades. And she couldn't write to save her life—maybe she had someone write her essay for her or something. If she did write her essay herself, she probably composed the whole thing on the keypad of her cell phone."

"Hmm." Sam took notes.

"The essay is really the hugest part of the contest. That's why it made no sense, her winning—even if they'd overlooked her grades. I worked forever on my essay. I kept asking Noelle about her essay topic, but she refused to even talk about it." She paused to slather herself with Coppertone.

"It doesn't sound like you miss her that much," I said.

"Of course I do," she said indignantly. "She was my best friend."

"Oh," I said. "Of course."

"Well, thanks for talking to us," Sam said. "It's been really helpful."

Lacey smiled at us. I'd never seen her look so happy. "Anytime! See you at the Rose Parade! I'll wave to you from my float."

Sam walked me back to the concessions stand.

"Maybe Lacey eliminated Noelle so that she could be Rose Queen," I suggested.

"Can you really imagine Lacey doing that? How would she do it—attack Noelle with a nail file? Smother her to death in sunscreen?"

I shrugged. "It's possible."

"Just to be queen of some ridiculous parade?"

I poured us Sprites. "I know we haven't lived in Venice that long, but in case you haven't noticed, this town seems more obsessed with that parade than New York was with the Subway Series. It's kind of scary."

Sam nodded. "That's true."

"Though you're right: Lacey doesn't seem like much of a murderer. And, uh, nice idea with the bathtub drain stoppers. If she had a 3.7 at school, I'm going to be valedictorian."

Henry stepped out from the kitchen. He didn't look happy. "You," he said to me. "You're over your break time by fifteen minutes!"

"It's my fault," Sam told him. "We were—I was distracting her."

Henry made a snorting noise and briskly swept the floor. "Your sister, your lifeguard boyfriend—you need to focus a little more on serving fries, young lady."

"He's not my boyfriend," I told Henry. "He's gross."

"Now he's gross," Henry said, and shook his head. "I'm sure you'll find another distraction real soon."

Sam decided to stay at work late that night—she wanted to research our list of suspects on the Internet to get more information about them. I needed a break, so I biked to the Petal Diner and sat by myself at the counter.

"You okay, hon?" Wilda asked me.

"I guess," I said. I could've really gone for a bowl of matzo-ball soup like the kind they serve at the Second Avenue Deli, with the matzo balls as big as your head, but of course they didn't serve that at the Petal. I ordered a burger and a chocolate milk shake.

"Man trouble?" she asked.

I smiled. "Sort of." I'd just been feeling a little shaken up by everything that had happened lately. The police and Gus investigating us and the prospect of us getting caught. A part of me worried that at any time Callowe or

Alby or Gus might march through that door and tell us that they'd figured out who we really were. Or that Enid would find us. That Sam and I might be separated and never see each other again. That was my biggest fear, and I couldn't seem to get it completely out of my head.

"I know how it is," Wilda said. "I heard about you and Troy."

"It's not just Troy, though. It's everything. Your friend Gus, too—I guess you know he's investigating us. I mean, does he—do people really think we did something to Noelle?"

She waved her hand. "Welcome to life in a small town. Don't worry about Gus—he's harmless. And Alby and Callowe and Troy and Noelle—all these people who are bothering you—it's just because you and your sister are new to them and different. You two are the smartest and funniest and prettiest things to come to this town in years. That's why everyone's giving you so much trouble."

"I guess not everyone's giving us trouble," I acknowledged. "I don't know what we'd do without you to cheer us up." I also thought of Fern and Chester and Colin. Especially Colin.

"I'm just glad you and your sister came here," Wilda said with a shrug. "You know my daughter, Rosa—she's thirty-three now—she left town as quick as she could, moved to Los Angeles and became a big-time lawyer and hasn't been back since."

"Really? Do you go out there to see her?" I'd never heard her talk about her daughter before.

Wilda picked up the saltshaker and stared at it

closely. "I've been out there a few times. Even thought of moving there, to be near my daughter and her husband. But I don't really fit in out there. This is my home. This is where I was born, where I work, where I'll probably die. Rosa left and she never looked back. She says there's nothing to do here, and it's too far away, and, well, she just doesn't have the time to come back. I know she just thinks it's boring here."

It seemed like a shame that Rosa had this wonderful mother who she rarely saw. Families were hard to understand—it seemed to me that if you had a mother as great as Wilda, you should do everything you could to be near her, to help her, to be there for her. To let her be there for you. Though I was glad that Wilda was there for us.

"You must really miss her," I said.

She wiped off a glass case filled with doughnuts. "I do. I guess I think missing someone is just a way of loving them. I know I love her, and she loves me. It's just that the way things worked out, we can't be together right now."

I nodded. It cheered me up a little to think of it that way. I felt like I'd spent my whole life missing people—my mom, and now my dad, and Vivien and all my friends from home. *Missing them is just a way of loving them,* I thought so I'd remember it.

Thirteen

Sam came back at nine that night. She put her jacket down on the kitchen table and microwaved a Stouffer's tuna noodle casserole. "I was on the computer the whole time," she said. "I did a little research into the McBrides' financial situation—I researched the Venice Bank and McBride Management, Noelle's father's company, which apparently owns most of the commercial buildings in town. I found a bunch of articles about McBride Management—and guess what? They've been having financial problems."

"So what does that have to do with Noelle disappearing?" I asked.

"I'm not exactly sure. But it's something I wonder about," Sam said. "I'm going to look into it some more."

In the meantime we decided that the next day at work, we'd have a little talk with Tara and Claire and find out what they knew. During our lunch break they were lying out by the pool. Sam came by to meet me, and we brought them two iced coffees.

Everything about them was similar—the round shape of their faces, the darkness of their tans; their colored contacts were the same shade of green. They looked like they'd just stepped out of a teenage-girl clone machine. I wondered if they timed themselves in the sun perfectly so that one didn't roast any more than the other.

"We were talking to Lacey yesterday about Noelle," Sam said. "She probably told you—"

"Yeah, we heard. You're trying to find Noelle yourselves," Claire said, twirling her ponytail. "I wish we knew what happened to her."

"It's just so awful," Tara said. "It's like the whole world's changed. I mean, we come here every day and some people actually try to *sit* in Noelle's *lounge chair*. I mean, God! It's *so* disrespectful."

"Lacey's already talking about taking over her place in the parade," I said.

"That's different, though," Claire said. "Lacey deserves to be queen, too."

"I wish we could be more help." Claire shrugged. "We just don't know anything. I mean, I keep thinking, where would Noelle go? She talked about going to Hollywood sometimes to become a movie star or pop singer or game-show assistant, but I'm pretty sure she was going to wait till she graduated high school."

"She didn't run away," Tara said. "I'm sure she didn't. She'd never miss being queen. And ditch her car like that? She *loved* that car. She loved it so much, she never even liked to drive it—she always had us or her parents give her rides. Also, her mom said she left all her makeup at home—if she was running away, she'd definitely take her makeup."

"I think something weird happened to her," Claire said. "Like my mom says, we can only hope she's okay."

"Who do you think might have been responsible for

her disappearance?" Sam asked them.

Tara stared at Claire, then they both turned to us, their expressions uneasy.

"We didn't have anything to do with it," I said. "That's why we're trying to help find her."

Tara stirred her drink. "I really can't think of anyone else. That's the problem. Except maybe that icky guy Noelle used to date."

"You're talking about Greg Burnville, right?" Sam asked.

They nodded and made faces at the mention of his name, as if he was the Antichrist.

"Anyone else?" Sam asked. "Teachers from school or acquaintances or—?"

They shook their heads.

"I hope you find her," Claire said. "It's just not the same without her here."

"I know," Sam said. "I hope we find her soon."

That night, during another game of Lorna Scrabble in Colin's shop, Colin, Sam, and I talked about how we'd approach Greg.

"*Harnso*. A rare breed of bison found only in North Dakota. I mean, should we just call Greg up randomly, do you think?" Sam asked.

"I know him a little from school. He's kind of a strange guy—sort of mean, actually. I bet he'd talk to you if you told him you liked his music, though. I have that CD from his band, Dog Breath, around here somewhere. Maybe you can tell him you're Dog Breath groupies," Colin said.

He looked at his letters and arranged them on the board. "*Dopein*. A chemical in the brain that causes extreme stupidity—Troy's known to have an excess of it."

"I think you should just go on a date with Greg," I told Sam. "I hear it's a really great, fun way to gather information." It was my turn. "*Wharla*. A Gaelic word for an overbearing older sister."

Colin went to look for Dog Breath's first and only CD and played it for us. "It's called *Candied Death*," he said. It was like listening to a whole lot of cars getting fixed in a mechanic's shop. You could hardly make out the country twang vocals over the din of bizarre noises in the background. Who knew there was such a thing as punk country music? Apparently Greg was a trail-blazer.

"Turn it off, please," Sam said after a while. "*Codfoy*. British slang for horrible music you have to pretend to like."

After our game Colin called Greg up and told him that he had two friends who loved his music and wanted to meet him. We agreed that the three of us would visit Greg in his garage the next afternoon.

Greg wore a sleeveless, ripped black T-shirt; he would've been handsome if it hadn't been for his mullet haircut and circles as dark as coal under his eyes.

"I'm glad you liked that disc," he told us. "The new one we're working on, *Blood and Tofu*—it's even better."

"*Blood and Tofu*?" I asked. I wasn't sure I'd heard right.

"Yeah. It's a metaphor."

I didn't ask for what. I didn't really want to know. We

talked about music for a while, and then Sam brought up Noelle. He had plenty to say about her.

"She's evil, man, I'm telling you. Worse than Yoko Ono!" He had a habit of strumming a chord on his guitar after every few sentences. "She was just bad, bad news." *Strum.* "Hot body, though. If only that head wasn't attached to it. I wrote this song about her. It's called 'I Hate You in the Night, I Hate You in the Morning.'"

"That sounds nice," Sam said.

He sang a bar for us.

> *I hate you in the night,*
> *I hate you in the morning.*
> *I hate you when it's light,*
> *I hate you 'cause you're boring.*

Then came the chorus:

> *Noelle sucks! Noelle sucks!*

"That's beautiful," Sam said.

"I'm *verklempt*," I said.

"She means—she's very kept," Sam said, giving me a warning look. "That's something we say in Cleveland."

"Yeah, it's total *codfoy*," Colin said.

"What?" Greg asked.

"*Codfoy*—British slang for great music," he explained. I had to fake a cough to cover my giggle.

"Thanks." Greg smiled. "Yeah, I just needed an outlet for all my feelings about Noelle. You know, she *completely*

ruined a record deal I had in the works with Tiger Records—
that Nashville label?—a couple of months ago." *Strum*.

"What happened?" Sam asked.

"The head of the label—Johnny Parsons—asked us
to send in a demo, and Noelle offered to mail it for us.
And you know what she did? She stuck in her own demo
instead! And a cheesy photo of herself, too." *Strum*.

"Parsons called in a rage, asking me what the sick joke
was. I said what? He'd gotten *Noelle*'s photo and demo
tape instead of Dog Breath's. What a megalomaniac! Hey,
that would be a good song title. '*Megalooomaniaaac.*' I
like that." He made a note to himself on a song sheet.

"I think Parsons was so upset because of Noelle's
voice. She's got delusions that she's the next Madonna,
but have you ever heard her? God." He shuddered. "It's
an abomination of the human vocal cords." *Strum*. "I
apologized up and down to Parsons, but after that whole
mess the deal fell apart. I know it was Noelle's fault. She
couldn't just sit back and let me have some success. But
at least I got the last laugh—did you see Parsons at the
club on karaoke night? Well, he only came because I told
him Noelle would be singing, if he wanted a laugh. I'm
sure he told her how awful she was to her face."

Greg seemed to have plenty of motive to want
Noelle to disappear, though he had an airtight alibi:
Dog Breath had had a gig in Indianapolis that night. He
hadn't come back to Venice until the following day.

We thanked him for talking to us and told him we
couldn't wait to come to his next show.

"I don't know," Sam said as we piled back into

Colin's car. "I just don't feel like we're making much progress in finding her. It's harder than I thought."

I wondered what our dad would do. His cases were always so cut-and-dried—someone trying to defraud an insurance company. Usually he just had to sit in the surveillance van and videotape people's front doors, waiting for them to come out and show some evidence that they weren't as injured as they said they were. It was amazing how much you could find out about a person just from watching them or looking in their windows. People having affairs, cheating on each other, doing all sorts of things they thought no one else knew about. And people do the funniest things when they think no one's looking—pick their noses extensively, scratch their butts, have entire conversations with themselves or their pets.

"Maybe we should just do surveillance on Noelle's house for a little while," I said.

"I guess we should try everything," Colin said. "When are we going to do it?"

"*We* are not doing it," Sam said. "Sophie and I will do it ourselves. We're not dragging you into any more trouble." She gave me another hard stare.

"I can help you guys, though," he said.

"No." Sam was firm. "Also, it will be easier for two people to sneak around than three. Besides, you're too tall. Not so good for prowling around unnoticed."

"Shaggy and Fred on *Scooby-Doo* seem pretty tall," I said.

"Sophie? Here's a word for you: *cartoon,*" she said.

Colin dropped us off at our house, and over dinner Sam said, "I hope he doesn't start to wonder how we actually know about surveillance and detective work."

"I know," I said. It was strange that we had this whole side of ourselves that we couldn't share with him. He was becoming a close friend, but he had no idea who we really were. I wished we could just tell him.

"We can't get him into trouble," Sam said.

I nodded. I longed for the day when we could just have friends without having to worry about them becoming accomplices to our crimes.

We decided we would begin the surveillance the following night.

I wished we had the van from our dad's company—it had tinted windows and a small lounge chair and cushions in back. I used to lie down and read magazines all day and watch the people out the window. Instead we had to use our growling, ancient car, which smelled like old cigarettes and musty upholstery. We wore the same black clothing we'd worn the night we followed Troy, except I'd added a black sweater. We stared at the house's huge white columns. Through the enormous dining-room windows we could see the McBrides eating dinner. We sat in the car for over an hour, watching them with binoculars. No one seemed to notice us parked there. At nine o'clock the McBrides put on their jackets and headed to their car.

"I don't know," I said when they were out of sight. "It doesn't seem like we're making any progress. I think we should get closer."

"I knew you would say that," Sam said. She opened up her knapsack. Inside were two small flashlights. "Let's go inside."

"Are you serious?" I guess I shouldn't have been surprised that my sister was so ready and willing to break the law—after all, she'd recently stolen three hundred thousand dollars that was legally Enid's and conceived of the whole idea for our new lives. Still, we'd never done anything like breaking and entering before.

"We'll be fast," she said. "You find Noelle's room, and I'll find Mr. McBride's office. You can look for anything that might give a clue as to what happened to her, and I'm going to take a peek at the McBrides' financial records."

"Okay," I said. My heart raced. I couldn't believe we were actually going to do this.

We got out of the car and were extra careful not to be seen, moving around and behind the house and then creeping along bushes and weeping willow trees onto the back of the McBrides' property.

Sam brought out a credit card to try to pick the lock of the back door as we walked onto the porch. She nervously inspected the lock. "I've never done this before."

"Are you sure it's locked?" I turned the knob, and the door opened. Small towns were great. I didn't know why there were so many thieves in New York City when you could break in with no hassle out here. Colin had often made fun of us for locking our door at night, but clearly you never knew when a Jewish orphan-girl detective might want to get into your house.

We slunk inside with our two tiny flashlights, walking through the living room and up the stairs. The house was ornately furnished in a kind of stuffy, museumlike way. Upstairs, we passed one small, nondescript bedroom that looked like a guest room—and then we saw Noelle's room. You couldn't miss it: a huge promo poster for this year's parade of Noelle in a Rose Queen tiara was on the wall beside her bed. The entire room was as pink as a Hostess Sno Ball. Sam wished me luck and slunk off in search of Mr. McBride's office.

I searched Noelle's room quickly. She didn't have many books—just shelves and shelves of Cliff's Notes—and there was no computer and no diary, both of which I'd hoped to find. I decided to take a clue from Gus and go through her garbage. I found the can, but it was empty.

I searched through dresser drawers and shelves and finally looked through her closet—I'd never seen so many shoes. They were hideous—dyed-to-match pumps in scary colors, turquoise sandals with huge bows, lavender cowboy boots, green suede ankle boots with fringe. Yikes. Then I looked through her handbags. She had about twelve. Most were ugly, but there was one large black Coach one. Ooh. Really nice. Must've been a gift. I wondered if she'd notice if it was missing.

On the closet shelf I found her notebook from school. Geometry, history, English. Her handwriting was bubbly, and she dotted her *i*'s with hearts. Lacey, Tara, and Claire had all scribbled *I love you, Noelle!* and *BFF* on the cover. Ugh. I wanted to barf. Nestled in the back pocket I found her report card from the spring semester—she'd actually had a 2.9 average. Hmm. There were some bits of crumpled paper inside the pocket, too. I uncrumpled them. They were scribbled notes from Tara and Claire—all about what color bikinis they would buy for the summer.

Nothing very helpful. I went back and picked up the black Coach bag. It looked like she'd hardly ever used it—such a shame. Inside I found a card—*Congratulations on Another Great School Year! Love, Mother*—and a letter, folded up and stashed deep inside the pocket.

> Dear Ms. McBride:
>
> Thank you for your interest in the 2003 Rose Queen contest. I regret to inform you that due to the impressive talent pool for this year's competition, your application was not selected. However, I wish you the best of luck and hope you enjoy all of this year's Rose Festival activities.
>
> Sincerely,
> Nancy Weller
> Mayor of Venice

It was dated June 9—over two months ago.

I put the letter in my pocket and went to find Sam. She was in Mr. McBride's office upstairs. She had the filing cabinet open alongside his desk.

"Did you find something?" she asked.

"Look at this." I showed her the letter.

She shook her head. "So Lacey was right. Something

strange *was* going on with that contest."

"Did you find anything?" I asked Sam.

"The McBrides are in debt," she said. "McBride Management has been operating at a loss for four quarters. So I can't imagine he'd use his money to buy his daughter some Rose Queen title." She tilted her head—there was a noise from outside. We clicked our flashlights off and listened to the crunch of wheels on gravel. I peeked out the window: a police car was pulling into the front driveway.

"Oh God," Sam said hoarsely. "I don't believe this."

We ran down the stairs and toward the back porch. I heard a knock on the front door just as we slipped out the back. We made a beeline for the nearest hedge and crept behind it, taking a roundabout route toward our car. My legs shook so much, I almost thought they'd collapse.

We reached the car without anyone seeing us, and from there we watched Alby walk around the house to the back and knock on that door. He checked the outside of the house, shining his huge flashlight in the windows. I held my hands in my lap, but they wouldn't stop quivering.

Sam turned the key in the ignition; the car growled loudly but didn't start. Alby looked up abruptly at the noise of the engine chugging.

"Let's go! He's seen us!" I yelled at Sam. "Hit the gas!"

"I am!" she screamed.

But our trusty Buick growled again and went dead.

fourteen

Alby stroked his peach-fuzz mustache. "Now, I'd really like to hear what you were doing parked outside the McBrides' house. I was driving by there and I saw a light upstairs, but nobody was home. Then I saw you. It's a very strange coincidence, I think," he said.

I was becoming uncomfortably familiar with the back of Alby's squad car. I didn't say anything; I hoped Sam could come up with a good explanation.

"We didn't do anything except park on a quiet street in Venice," Sam barked in her older-sister voice. "You have no reason to bring us in for questioning."

Alby looked a little uncomfortable. "Well, my brother's going to want to talk to you," he said weakly.

The police station was also becoming familiar. The Rose Parade posters on the walls, the little statue of a gondolier in the lobby, the coffee room where Alby and Callowe questioned us some more. I took off my black sweater and put it on the chair, realizing that my T-shirt was damp with sweat.

"Can you please fill me in on why you were parked outside the McBrides' house?" Callowe asked, tapping his fingers on the table.

"We wanted to talk to the McBrides," Sam said.

"We're tired of everyone suspecting us of something we had nothing to do with. We decided to ask them a few questions, see if we could help find out the truth somehow. They weren't home, so we waited outside for a while, thinking they might return soon."

"My brother saw a light on in their house. A flashlight, you thought, right, Alby?"

Alby nodded. "I think maybe it was."

"Think maybe?" Callowe asked.

"Well—I was driving up, and it was all sort of fast. And then the girls were there, so I thought . . . well, I thought you'd want to talk to them."

How much more trouble were Sam and I going to get into over this whole Noelle mess? Granted, we had broken into the McBrides' house. But we were making a lot more progress in this investigation than the police were.

"Listen, we know that there was something strange going on with the Rose Queen contest this year," I told him. "Maybe *that's* what you should be turning your attention to instead of coming after us."

"What are you talking about?" Alby asked.

"Apparently Noelle was selected by inappropriate, illegitimate means," Sam said.

Callowe—bored, suspicious Callowe—looked like we'd just slapped him in the face. He turned bright red.

"All right, enough. I've had enough of you two for a while. I don't want to see you back here again. Stay away from the McBrides and their house, or it's going to be trouble." He hustled us out of the coffee room in a hurry.

"What was that about?" Sam said as we left the station. "What made him so upset?"

"I don't know." It was getting cold outside; I shivered. Callowe had ushered us out so quickly that I'd left my sweater on the chair in the coffee room. I told Sam to wait for a minute while I went back for it. She said she'd call Colin and see if he could pick us up.

Callowe's office was right next door to the coffee room. I could hear muffled yelling coming out of it. I grabbed my sweater and listened by the door. He was on the phone with someone. What was he so mad about? I looked around the hallway to make sure no one was nearby and listened more closely.

"I always knew this would come back to get us. I told you I didn't want to get involved in this kind of thing. I told you that! I always thought it was a bad idea; she was just a teenage girl, after all, and now it's hanging over our heads . . . I wish you'd just go ahead and get a damn divorce, you know? It's the twenty-first century, for God's sake. Who's going to care? Who's really going to care?"

I pressed my ear against the wall, trying to hear more, but Callowe's voice sank in pitch and I couldn't make out more words. Alby stepped out of another room and into the hall, and I quickly walked out behind him. As I loped through the station lobby, I knocked against the gondolier statue. It fell on the floor—and bounced without breaking, thankfully—but Callowe heard the noise and bolted out of his office. We locked eyes. His nostrils flared with anger, and I fled out the door as fast as I could.

*　　*　　*

Colin picked us up outside the police station.

"I can't believe you broke into their house," he said. He shook his head.

"Well, at least we've finally made some progress." Sam filled him in on everything we'd found—the note from the mayor and the McBrides' financial situation. "The fact that the McBrides are in financial trouble explains why the only investigator they could afford was Gus," she said.

"That's not all, either," I said. I told them what I'd overheard Callowe saying. "Do you think Callowe could've done Noelle in?" I asked. "He got so angry when we mentioned the Rose Queen contest being suspicious. And then on the phone—'she *was* just a teenage girl,' he said." I shuddered. "I always thought there was something kind of creepy about him. I bet he did it."

"I don't know if he did it, but it definitely sounds like he's involved in some way . . . and he's having an affair with someone," Sam said.

"Yuck. The idea of Callowe having an affair with anyone is not an image I want in my mind," I said.

"I know." She laughed. "It's pretty disturbing."

"He's about as sexy as a barnacle," I said.

"Or a harnso," Colin said.

"A harnso would definitely be sexier than a Callowe," I said.

It was getting late, but we decided to go back to Colin's for some ice cream. We needed to relax after all the events of the night. Slumping down into Colin's cushiony sofa with a bowl of mint chocolate chip was exactly what I needed.

"I just wish I could make sense of this whole thing," Colin said. "Maybe there was a recount or something— and Noelle *did* win legitimately? Nancy doesn't seem like the type of person who'd take a bribe, especially over something like the Rose Queen contest. She's so down-to-earth. And she doesn't need the money—she's married to one of the richest guys in town."

Sam rolled her eyes. "Oh, please. I know you think the mayor's great, but it seems pretty obvious that something out of the ordinary is going on."

I looked around Colin's shop at all the little figurines on the shelves. Like a funky Hallmark store.

"Hey, do you remember the first time we met the mayor, what she bought when she came to the shop?" I asked. "Wasn't it some weird little tchotchke stuff?"

"She always buys these cheesy little ceramic animal things," Colin said. "She goes crazy over those."

"And you know how many cheesy little ceramic animals Callowe has all over his desk?"

"Wait. I keep a sales log," Colin said. He got up and started flipping through the books, listing the mayor's purchases out loud. Apparently she had bought enough ceramic figurines to populate a whole ceramic village. He described frogs, mice, bunnies—and a cow playing the bagpipes.

"I saw that on his desk," I blurted. "She must have given it to him. And I bet it wasn't just an innocent thank-you-for-your-campaign-contribution gift . . ."

"So maybe Noelle found out about the mayor's affair with Callowe," Sam said slowly. "Maybe she used it to blackmail the mayor into making her queen of the Rose Parade. And maybe Callowe got rid of her to make sure she never talked . . ."

"I don't know," Colin said. "I can't picture either of them *murdering* Noelle. It just seems . . . well . . . far-fetched."

I wanted to say, *All right, corn-fed midwestern boy, people really do get murdered.* There was an earnestness about Colin, and a lot of the people we'd met in Indiana, that I'd never found in New York. In New York you just expected every stranger to be a murderer. Pretty ironic, too, considering it was here in Indiana that my mother had been murdered—not in the big bad city of New York. But I couldn't say any of this, because we were supposedly from the Midwest, too.

"I think it's very possible that either of them could've done it," Sam said. "And it's another reason for us to be even more careful now. We might have a real murder here. And Callowe might know that you overheard him, Sophie. And someone who got rid of one troublesome teenage girl would have no qualms about getting rid of a couple more."

"I think you two are watching too much TV. Remember this is Venice, not Cleveland," Colin said.

We finished our ice cream and said good night to him, then walked back home. I couldn't stop shivering the whole way back, even in my sweater.

fifteen

The next morning I sat on the living-room couch, eating Cheerios and zoning out on mindless TV, trying not to think about the possibility that the police chief of Venice was going to try to murder me. Then suddenly my head jerked up as I realized there *was* someone pretty scary who probably wanted to kill me right now—my boss, Henry. I'd told him I'd come in that day to cover for him even though I was supposed to have the day off, since it was his son's birthday party. I should have been at work already. I put on my flip-flops, gathered my things, said good-bye to Sam, ran out the door, and biked faster than I ever had before. I showed up at the club breathless, my hair waving all over the place.

"I'm so sorry," I said. "I just forgot—"

He leaned against the deep fryer, his arms crossed. "This is the last straw, Fiona. I've had it. You're fired."

"Henry—please, I'm really sorry—"

"No. I don't want to hear any more of it. You're always off on breaks, talking to your sister or the boys, or else you're at the police station, from what I hear."

"But—"

"Enough," he said.

I left the club feeling like I had lead weights attached

to my feet. How was I going to explain this one to Sam? I decided to bike around a little—I didn't feel like going home right away, and I needed some time to think. I pedaled slowly through the winding streets of town and then through the deserted old industrial area that edged the outer reaches of the canal. I liked this part of Venice; it reminded me a little bit of Long Island City in Queens—the Silvercup Studios building and the old Chiclets factory and all those boxy warehouses.

That's when I saw the police car.

It turned a corner and started to cruise slowly toward me. My heart pounded; my arms felt weak. There was no one else on the street. I was completely alone. I turned around and started to bike away from the police car as fast as I could, but it pulled up beside me and the window glided down. Callowe looked at me from the driver's seat, his face expressionless behind his mirrored sunglasses.

"A young girl like you shouldn't be by herself, biking alone in this part of town," he said. His voice sounded lower and meaner than usual—it was gravelly and cold. I thought of my mom. I hated thinking about what the last moments of her life had been like, but sometimes I couldn't help it.

I pedaled away from him as fast as I could—I headed toward a narrow alley a block away, biking for my life, certain that if Callowe caught me, he'd kill me in whatever way he'd killed Noelle. Energy surged through me from out of nowhere; my muscles seemed stronger than they ever had. I biked furiously down the alley, around a corner, down another alley, and along a sidewalk.

And smack into Gus Jenkins.

It seemed to happen in slow motion. I saw him walking down the street and swerved to miss him but caught the edge of his leg; I fell off the bike and hit the ground, and Gus lay spread-eagled on the sidewalk.

"Uuuuuuh," he moaned. "Ohhhhhhh."

"Oh God." I stood up; my cheek stung and I had blood on my hands, but Gus looked worse than I felt.

He clutched his knee. "Are you trying to kill me?"

"No! Someone's trying to kill me!" I flailed my arms like a crazy person. I saw the police car reach the corner and pause, and then continue straight ahead. As I watched Callowe's car disappear, my entire body felt like it was about to melt into the sidewalk, I was so relieved. "You just saved my life," I said to Gus through panting breaths.

Gus stuck out his hand. "Help me up." I did; he straightened, leaning on me, and rubbed his head. Then he squinted at me and reached out to touch my face. "You're bleeding. We gotta get you cleaned up."

We were outside Muther's, a seedy-looking bar. Gus took me inside, and Jared, the bartender, gave me a clean soft towel to take into the bathroom.

I was a mess. The skin on my right cheekbone below my eye was completely gone. All that remained was a bloody red welt. My lip was bleeding, too, and I'd scraped half the skin off my knee. I shuddered. Would I be scarred for life? Could I cover it up with makeup? Now I'd really never have a boyfriend, looking like this.

I wiped off all the blood and washed the scratches

off my hands, elbows, and legs. I looked at my hands under the running water; they were still shaking.

When I walked back out into the bar, I started crying. I couldn't help it; I was too unnerved.

"Calm down, it's okay," Gus said. He patted my shoulder awkwardly, which made me sob more. Finally he just hugged me.

"He was gonna kill me," I murmured into Gus's chest. "I thought—"

"It's okay," Gus said. "Jared, thanks—I think I'll let her calm down next door." I wiped my nose, and Gus brought me to his office, which was in an old factory building next to the bar. The room looked like a tornado had blown through it. I'd never seen such a mess. Piles and piles of papers, old notebooks, McDonald's takeout bags, and crushed beer and soda cans lay everywhere. I had to step over a broken file box overflowing with receipts just to get to the chair, and I had to move a clump of clothes from the chair to sit down.

Gus looked a little embarrassed by the mess. "I— uh—I'm between secretaries at the moment." He patted his pockets.

At least I'd stopped crying. There was something kind of fatherly and protective about him. When he'd hugged me, it felt a little bit like my dad's hugs—like I could just be in his arms and everything would be okay. In most ways Gus seemed nothing like our dad— our dad was thin and intellectual and hardly ever drank, except for the occasional whiskey sour and a few glasses of Manischewitz wine at Passover. Gus was fat, burly, stubbly—a mess. But something about him made me feel safe.

"Now, make yourself comfortable—look out for that Coke bottle at your feet—and tell me who was trying to kill you. Before you practically killed me, that is."

Before I knew what I was saying, I poured out the whole story to him—how Sam and I were trying to solve the mystery to clear ourselves of suspicion, how we were certain that Callowe and the mayor had murdered Noelle, how we worried that our lives were in danger now.

Gus listened calmly and at the end of my speech handed me the phone. "Call your sister," he said. "We need to talk."

Sam arrived, her face flushed. "Sophie—oh my God!" She hugged me. "Are you okay? We should go to the emergency room, get you checked out—" She brushed my hair from my face.

"I'm fine," I said. "It's just a scrape." I arranged several wisps of hair back over my right eye—I'd been practicing that in Gus's bathroom mirror; if I did my hair just the right way, it covered up the huge red splotch beneath my eye.

"How did this happen?"

I started to fill her in on Callowe's attempt to murder me, but Gus interrupted. "Now let's try and be realistic for a second, here. I've known Callowe for fifteen years, and he's not the type of man who would make a career out of abducting and eliminating teenage girls. I think there's some misunderstanding. I could picture him having a, uh, rendezvous with Mayor Weller—she's a fine-looking lady, I must say—but murder? Nah. I just don't see it."

"How do you know? Everyone keeps telling us things about people"—I thought of Difriggio telling us everything would be fine in Venice, that it was the perfect place for us, and now look at this mess we'd gotten in—"and why should we believe them? How do we know who to listen to?"

Gus rested his elbows on the stacks of papers on his desk. "I guess you don't. You've just got to listen to your gut and trust that. Maybe I'm wrong about Callowe. Maybe you're right. But on the off chance that you are right, I'm a little better equipped to deal with it than you two girls are. I think I should be the sole investigator from here on in."

"The sole investigator?" Sam asked. "What—you don't like us competing for your business? Or that we made so much more progress than you did?" She sounded incredibly angry and a little scared, too. "You can't even see your desk! You can't even see the floor in here. A murderer could be in this very room and you wouldn't find him."

Gus's lips formed a thin line, but he nodded; there was simply no denying that there was some truth to this.

"I don't know," I said. "It seems like maybe *you* could use *our* help. We could work together—you could keep an eye on Callowe and on us, and I could help you out with all this." I waved at the clutter around the room. "You said you need a secretary. And I need a job."

"You have a job," Sam said.

I smiled at her awkwardly. "Um—not exactly." I told her how Henry hadn't been very understanding when I'd shown up late for work. For the moment I was almost thankful that I was bruised, since she didn't seem particularly angry.

"I don't know," Gus said. "I'd have to see your résumé and qualifications." I wasn't sure if he was joking or not. "Though I hear from Difriggio that you're pretty trustworthy," he added with a sly grin.

Sam and I exchanged looks. What exactly had Difriggio told Gus about us? Had he figured out any part of our secret? We'd have to call Difriggio and find out how much Gus actually knew.

"How about you just leave things to me for now, and I'll keep you posted on the status of the investigation," Gus said.

"We'll think about it," Sam said. I nodded. I was a little worn-out from all this detective work, especially after the events of the day.

We called Difriggio on the way home.

"No, of course I didn't let anything out that would put him onto you," Difriggio said. "What do you take me for, an amateur?" I smiled, thinking of Felix using that line—now I knew where he'd learned it. "I don't reveal clients' privileged information to *anyone*," Difriggio went on. "Like I said before, I told him I'd known your parents a long time ago, and that's it. But remember—Gus isn't always as bumbling as he looks. There's a shrewd mind attached to that out-of-shape body. I wouldn't be surprised if he suspected something was up. Of course, who knows if he can stay sober long enough to follow any hunch of his through."

This gave us some relief. Sam also filled Difriggio in about the current state of the whole Noelle situation. He said to hang tight for now, and Sam took notes for a while about what to do if things really got bad—then we might need to relocate and start this whole ordeal all over again.

We spent the rest of the afternoon at the drugstore, purchasing cover-up products for my face. At home I stood in our bathroom, applying Cover Girl foundation, Revlon concealer, and Maybelline pressed powder on top of the welt. Medically, it was probably best to let the wound breathe, so to speak, but I didn't care. I just wanted to look normal. I kept thinking, as I styled and restyled my hair, that despite everything that had happened lately, I didn't want to leave Venice. It was beginning to feel sort of like home. We had Colin, Wilda, Chester, Ethel, Fern, and now Gus on our side. In my gut, I trusted all of them. I didn't want to pack up and move and start all over again from scratch. Once was enough.

Sixteen

Even though we were expecting Colin for dinner that night, I still checked the peephole twice before letting him in. Once I finally opened the door, he took a long look at my face and his jaw dropped. "What happened to you?" he asked.

I sighed; my attempts at concealing obviously hadn't been as effective as I'd hoped. I filled him in and showed him the bike. The paint was chipped, the handlebars dented, and the basket in front was broken in half. "It could have been worse," he said. "God, I'm glad you're okay. Your first bike wreck, I take it?"

I nodded.

He gave me a hug. "You'll both be looking like new in no time."

We ate macaroni and cheese, with brownies for dessert, half wondering if we should expect Callowe to show up at our door any minute to abduct us. After the brownies, while we were sipping tea, there was a knock on the door. We all flinched—but it was Gus.

A faint bourbon smell followed Gus into the room; I figured he'd made a stop at Muther's on his way over. I hoped that he wouldn't mention anything about Difriggio in front of Colin. Thankfully, Gus seemed completely friendly and relaxed, although pretty tipsy.

"I've done some poking around. Thought I'd tell you about it so you didn't sit here worrying all night long that Callowe was going to come burn down your house."

"We're not worried," I lied.

"Yeah. Good. Well, it turns out Callowe and Nancy both have strong alibis for the night Noelle disappeared. After the karaoke Nancy spent the night with her husband at a hotel in Indianapolis, since they had a fund-raising breakfast there first thing the next morning. Callowe ate a bad corn dog at a 7-Eleven after he left karaoke and spent the rest of the night puking his brains out in the bathroom of his house, where he still lives with his mother and brother."

"So we were completely wrong about them?" Sam asked.

"They're not murderers, but you're right about one thing," Gus said. "Maybe I'm not the most organized, but I know a few things about detective work. I got Callowe to talk. I still got my techniques. I can put the pressure on when the situation calls for it. And this is what I found out—he and Nancy Weller are having an affair. Hot and heavy, from what I gather."

"Spare us the seedy details," Sam said. "We just ate."

He nodded. "When I pressed Callowe, he admitted it—and he also admitted, after much embarrassment, that Noelle knew about the affair and used that information to pressure Nancy into making her Rose Queen. Callowe didn't want to give in to Noelle's pressure—he was okay with letting people know about the affair and so on and so forth—but Nancy didn't want the affair to be public knowledge, especially not with the election around the corner."

We sat there quietly, absorbing this new information.

"I did discover one more thing," Gus told us. He yawned and rubbed his sore knee. His eyelids began to droop. "Callowe and Nancy used to rendezvous at a little roadside motel in the next town over. I went over there to check things out. I showed the manager Noelle's picture to see if there was some connection between Noelle and the mayor and Callowe—maybe they had some meeting there or something about the blackmail. Well, the manager did recognize Noelle—but she hadn't come there to see Callowe or the mayor. She came in looking for another guest, a guy who wore a sparkly cowboy outfit. The manager didn't remember what the guy's name was, but apparently Noelle came to see him late on the night she disappeared—after midnight. Which was *after* you two girls dropped her off, am I correct?"

Sam and I nodded, reeling from this news. Sparkly cowboy outfit—we all knew who that was. "Johnny Parsons," Sam breathed.

"Do you think Johnny Parsons murdered Noelle?" I said. My voice was nearly a whisper. He'd seemed so harmless. Goofy and strange, but not violent. He had a pet squirrel, for God's sake. I felt sad all of a sudden, thinking that maybe there had been something we could've done to save Noelle's life. Maybe we should've realized he was dangerous.

"What should we do now?" I asked Gus, forgetting

that he didn't even know who Johnny Parsons was.

He didn't answer me. His head slowly tilted back toward the wall; his eyelids began to close.

"Is he okay?" Colin said.

"I think he had one drink too many," I said.

Soon Gus began to snore gently in his chair. We left him there, covered with a blanket, and did what Nancy Drew never could: turned on Sam's laptop and Googled Johnny Parsons on the Internet.

We found references to Johnny Parsons all over the Web. His record company, Tiger Records, had experienced a brief period of fame in Nashville, producing several hit songs and one country music star—until it had gone under eight weeks ago. According to the news articles we dug up from Nashville papers and in music industry magazines, the business had started to sour about six months ago. Parsons had lost interest in his company. Rumors abounded about him selling the label, but instead it just went defunct. Parsons himself disappeared completely from the Nashville scene. Two months ago he'd left town on a "scouting trip," one article said, and he'd simply never come back.

Sam couldn't find a current address for him on the Web. Several of the articles had mentioned the names of Parsons's business associates at Tiger Records. "Maybe we can contact them," I suggested.

We called information in Nashville and got a phone number for Leda Lang, a former executive producer for Tiger Records. After a minute of squabbling over who would make the phone call, Colin finally convinced us that he could probably do the best job of charming her. Sam and I listened in on the other extension.

"I'm doing a short piece on the rise and fall of Tiger Records for *Rolling Stone*," Colin explained to Leda. "I just wanted to ask you a few questions. We'd also like to get in touch with Johnny Parsons—we were hoping you'd be able to help us."

"Honey, I wish I could. I'd like to find him myself. He owes me a hell of a lot of money."

"Do you have any idea where he might be?"

"Honey, I don't know. He never talked about his home much, though I know he was from some itty-bitty town in Indiana somewhere. Don't even bother looking—we called every Parsons in the state of Indiana, and he's not any of them. He had no family left there—parents were dead—he wasn't married himself. All he had in the world was a much younger sister who was almost like a daughter to him. She was a great kid—a little brooding and strange, but a great kid. He practically raised that little girl—Laurel was her name—by himself, but he had a kinda tough relationship with her. She got wild and ran away about six months ago and was killed in a car accident. After that, Johnny was never the same. He lost interest in his business, started getting all weird. Now none of us can find him."

Colin asked her a few random questions about the record company and then said, "Well, thank you so much."

"Thank you, honey," Leda said.

"He must have come back home to Indiana," Sam

said. "To his family's place. But where are we going to find him?"

"Maybe we should start with the sister," I said. "There could be some reports of her running away or her death and funeral."

We looked all over Nashville and Indiana newspapers' Web sites, trying to find some mention of Laurel Parsons, but found nothing.

"It's like a wild-goose chase," I said. I was tired from staring over Sam's shoulder at the screen for so long. Apparently no one named Parsons had died in the state of Indiana around six months ago.

An idea started to grow in my mind, but I couldn't mention it to Sam with Colin in the room. The second he got up to go to the bathroom, I leaned in and whispered in Sam's ear: "Why not check that Web site where Enid posted our missing person's reports?"

Sam's eyebrows lifted, and she smiled. "Good idea," she said. "Go distract Colin when he comes out of the bathroom so I can do the search." The last thing in the world that we needed was for Colin to see the screen with Samantha and Sophia Shattenberg on it.

I waited for the sound of flushing and greeted Colin in the living room. "Hey—I wanted to show you this." It was the new Edna St. Vincent Millay biography, which I was reading. I'd ordered it from Amazon.com—at least, if I had to be a big-city runaway hiding in a small town, I was doing it during the age of Internet shopping.

"I've heard about that book. Maybe I can borrow it when you're done."

"It's great. It talks all about her free love and all that. She was really into free love."

"Huh, yeah." Colin shifted uncomfortably. "Free love," he said awkwardly.

We stood by the bookshelves for a while, looking at various poetry books together—I'd gotten most of them from his shop.

"Guys! Come here!" Sam yelled from the kitchen. "You're not going to believe this!"

While searching through the missing person's reports, Sam hadn't found a Laurel Parsons—but she'd found a Laurel Parsil. Last seen in Nashville; ran away six months ago; the case had been closed, the report said; unfortunately Laurel Parsil had been declared dead.

We came to another article. More of the same information about Laurel Parsil, but this one had a photo.

A shocking photo. The girl in the picture was Noelle.

Well, at least it was someone who looked uncannily like Noelle. She wore no makeup and had tousled, unbrushed hair; she wasn't quite as skinny as Noelle. Plus she was smiling authentically in the photo—something Noelle rarely did.

"This is so creepy," I said. "What's going on?"

Sam Googled Laurel Parsil, and several more articles came up. One of them was an obituary for her from Phillips, Indiana, her hometown. It said that Laurel's sole survivor was an older brother, Wendel Parsil, who was born and raised in Phillips but currently lived in Nashville.

"So Johnny Parsons is a made-up name. Why didn't Leda Lang tell us that?"

"Maybe she didn't know. Maybe he didn't tell people what his real name was for some reason."

I thought of us and how Colin didn't even know our real names. So much went on in people's private lives that others never knew.

"Why would he change his name so slightly, from Parsil to Parsons?" Colin asked.

"Who knows," I said. "Maybe he wanted to do Presley, but that was already taken."

"Or Parsley, but he didn't want to be associated with a garnish," Colin said.

"Guys," Sam said. "Focus. Where's Phillips?" she asked Colin.

"I don't know." He shrugged. "It must be tiny—I've lived in Indiana my whole life and I've never heard of it."

We got out an atlas and found Phillips on the map. It was a small blip about ninety miles from Venice.

Gus was still snoozing away, but we knew what we had to do. Sam wrote a quick note to Gus and left it on the kitchen table. The three of us jumped into Colin's car and set off for Phillips.

We arrived just before midnight. The problem was, there hardly was any Phillips, especially at that hour. I couldn't believe a town smaller than Venice could exist, but there it was. The entire town consisted of a Mobil station, the Phillips General Store, and Aggie's Pizza, which was closed. The houses were weathered gray clapboard, and farther down the road there were only mobile homes. Maybe Venice did deserve its name—compared to this town, it seemed like a fancy, exotic metropolis.

"What should we do?" I said. "Go back home?"

"I think we should stay here and wait till it's light, then continue our search first thing in the morning," Colin said. "I have a tent in the back of my car—we can camp out."

We drove around and soon found a small grassy meadow. We were really in the middle of nowhere. Colin parked the car, and Sam and I helped him set up the tent.

Sam, who usually went to bed around ten-thirty, was exhausted. "I think I'm going to crash now."

"I'll join you in a little bit," I said. I wasn't tired at all; I was wired from all the excitement.

"We should start a fire," Colin said. "It'll keep us warm till we go to bed." I walked around and gathered some kindling, and he found some larger pieces of wood. He arranged the wood on top of some newspaper from his car and started a small fire. We sat around it, warming our legs, and stared up at the sky.

"What a crazy day." I shook my head and hugged my knees to my chest. "Actually, it's been pretty crazy ever since we moved here."

"You probably thought it was going to be a calm transition, coming from Cleveland."

I laughed. "Yeah. Calm." That was funny. I couldn't even remember what it felt like to actually be calm.

"Did your family go camping much?" he asked.

"What? Oh . . . no, not really."

"It's one of the nice things about life in the country." He leaned back against a large rock. "You know, it's strange—I feel like I've spent a bunch of time with you guys, but you hardly ever talk about Cleveland, or your friends back home, or any of that. I guess that's just because you miss it and your friends a lot, right?"

I felt like I'd just swallowed a brick. Why was he asking this? "Yeah. I miss everything. A lot—a real lot." I felt a little dizzy and could feel those old tears fighting their way up again. I wished more than anything that I could just let down my guard for once. I could feel all our secrets inside me, weighing me down, and I wanted more than anything to unburden my heart and tell Colin everything. But I knew I couldn't. I knew he could never know.

"You know what? I'm really getting tired all of a sudden. I think I should just get to sleep," I said.

"Oh. Okay," he said. I got up and went into the tent. I lay awake for a while, wondering if you could really have a close friendship with someone who didn't even know who you truly were. Colin must have sat outside by the fire for a long time, because when he came into the tent, I was fast asleep.

In the morning we packed up the tent and headed to the general store. We bought coffee and doughnuts and asked if anyone knew the Parsils and where they'd once lived.

"I know the Parsils," the old guy behind the register

said. "Sad, sad family. Mother dies, father dies, crazy son always listening to those records. Then the daughter. She died, you know, just this February."

"Do you know where they lived?" Sam asked. "We need to find Johnny—Wendel—and we were thinking if their home still existed—"

"Can't help you there. Parsil family home burned to the ground five years ago. Wendel still owns the land, far as I know—good chunk of acreage—but no one's seen him since his sister's funeral. He was all broken up about it, you know. Said it was his responsibility to keep his baby sister safe, and he'd failed her. Said he wished he'd locked his sister up so she couldn't run away. Sad, sad story."

Sam, Colin, and I exchanged glances.

We headed out to the Parsil family's old property, which was about three miles away, down a series of secluded back roads. We found the remains of the house: its scarred, blackened foundation and the ruins of its chimney rising into the air. We walked around the foundation; I tried to picture what it once had been like, when this house was still standing.

"Look at this," Colin said. Not far from the foundation were fresh tire tracks heading up an old, overgrown dirt driveway and into the woods.

We followed the tracks on foot—we didn't want Parsons to hear us coming and run off or attack us. We walked for about two or three miles, until we came upon a tiny, old, run-down shack. There was no car parked outside. But I did see a fat squirrel chattering loudly.

Its green glittery collar sparkled in the sun, and I could swear it had a stain of spaghetti sauce on its face.

"Look," I said, pointing. *"The squirrel."*

My skin froze. Parsons might be around somewhere nearby, and he could be dangerous. I stepped back slightly, closer to Colin and my sister.

They recognized the squirrel, too. I never knew a squirrel could be such a harrowing sight. "Let's be careful," Sam whispered. "Do you think he's around?"

Colin shook his head. "There's no car or bike here. I don't think he's here."

Then we heard something. It was a girl's very soft, quavery, off-key singing coming from inside.

"Noelle?" Sam said.

The singing stopped. "Hello?" the voice said after a pause. "Mom? Mom?"

Colin tried the door to the shed—a huge padlock hung from it, and there were no windows anywhere.

"Noelle—are you okay?" Sam asked loudly.

I heard soft sobs. "Help—please," she whimpered. She sounded so frightened and desperate, I almost felt sick. We rushed around the shed in a frenzy, looking for some way to break in. We couldn't find anything—the wood was solid, and there were no other doors. A woodpile stood in the distance, though—Colin walked over to it. A small ax sat beside it. He told Noelle to stand away from the door, and he hurled the ax into it.

Sam and I looked frantically around while Colin went to work chopping through the door; I prayed that Parsons wouldn't suddenly appear. "Hurry!" Sam shouted at him.

Finally he made a splintered hole in the door and told Noelle to climb through—the door was still padlocked and couldn't be opened. She stuck her arm through and then her shoulders and head. She was crying hysterically now, and I could see she was wearing a baggy peasant dress and a kerchief on her head—quite a switch from her poolside attire. Her hair looked like it hadn't been washed in a week—and without makeup or any of her usual clothes, she looked more like Parsil's sister than herself.

She kept crying and crying, and Colin held her in his arms like she was a child. "It's okay," he told her. "You're safe now. You're going to be fine. We have to get you out of here, though," and he looked at Sam, who took her hand, and we all started running down the path as fast as we could.

Epilogue

"I would've found her if you kids didn't need so much less sleep than me," Gus said, munching on a rose-petal-covered doughnut. "You little whippersnappers are gonna put us old-timers out of business."

"Less sleep? How about fewer drinks?" Sam asked him.

"Ah, I'm working on that," Gus said, starting in on his second doughnut.

"Those darn meddling kids," Colin said.

Gus didn't get the *Scooby-Doo* reference; he was a little too old for it. I didn't bother to explain.

We watched the pink floats and glittering baton twirlers swirl by in the parade. It had been two weeks since we'd found Noelle—and she still hadn't really returned to her old self. After we'd left Parsons's shed, we brought her to the police station, where her parents came to pick her up. No one saw her around town for a week after that—she just stayed inside, recovering from her ordeal.

On the way back from Phillips, Noelle had filled us in on what had happened. She told us that she'd first talked to Johnny at karaoke night and asked if he could make her a star. He told her to come speak with him at his hotel later that night. Naive, ambitious Noelle had eagerly gone, prepared to fend off romantic advances if necessary but not prepared for his lunacy. He'd told her that Nashville was no place for a decent young girl like her and that it was his mission to "keep her safe." He started ranting a bit, and it became clear that he was mistaking her for his own sister. She got scared and tried to leave; he stopped her, locked her in his car, drove her car into the nearby river, and whisked her off to the outbuilding at his parents' old home. He'd kept her in that shed ever since, apparently convinced that she was his little sister reincarnated, that God was giving him another chance to be a good guardian. She'd tried to get out, but he kept the place padlocked.

While Noelle was avoiding the public eye, her mother called to thank us.

"We don't know how to repay you," Mrs. McBride said. "If there's anything we can do for you anytime, please just ask."

"We're just glad she's okay," Sam said. When we'd told Difriggio what had happened, he'd said rescuing Noelle was one of the best things we could have done to ensure our identities were safe in Venice: we now had the most prominent, influential family in town—whether it had financial problems or not—owing us some huge favors. Difriggio had said that would certainly come in handy at some point in the future.

After Noelle's mother had spoken to us, she put Noelle on the phone. "I, um, wanted to thank you," Noelle said in a stiff voice.

"We're just glad you're fine," Sam said.

"Yeah, we're glad you're okay," I chimed in from the upstairs extension. Considering everything, I wasn't going to hold a grudge against her.

"Are you, um, going to tell everybody what I looked like when you found me?" Noelle asked.

"Don't worry," I said, since I knew I was the one that question was really directed at. "We won't tell anyone."

"Good." She sounded relieved. "I've never been so humiliated before." At least she seemed a little humbled by her experience. "Listen, if you want, you two can be my ladies-in-waiting on the Queen's Float at the parade."

"Oh, no thanks, that's okay," Sam and I said practically in unison.

The parade was the first time we had seen Noelle since the day we rescued her from Parsons's shed. She didn't seem quite so humble now—she was basking in her glory as co-queen with Lacey (the mayor had announced that they would share the position). Tara and Claire were the ladies-in-waiting. Though most of the town seemed to know that Noelle had attained her title through less than legitimate means, everyone seemed happy to see her back safely. Well, almost everyone—Greg was off skulking around the perimeters of the parade, shooting Noelle dark glares. And Troy seemed too busy to even notice Noelle was back—he was nuzzling a redheaded girl by the cotton-candy stand.

Sam and I had decided to look at the whole Parsons-Noelle case as a cautionary tale—we better not lose each other, like Parsons lost his sister, or we might just go nuts, abduct teenagers, and keep pet squirrels and feed them spaghetti.

The Rose Parade was unlike anything I'd ever seen before. Nearly everyone in town wore pink or red clothes and antenna headbands with roses on the ends. A crowd of kids from Venice Elementary were dressed up as every variety of rose imaginable, with different labels on their chests: American beauty, Polyantha, Floribunda, Grandiflora. The Venice Ladies' Choir whirled by on their pink float and led the crowd in a hearty rendition of "Rose, Rose, Rose Your Boat." Even the dogs were wearing pink, including Troy's dog, Fonzie, who had on a pink jacket. Isabel, Fern's poodle, actually had rosebuds tied to the bows around her ears.

All the stores of downtown had tables out; various food stands sold Rose Doughnuts, Rose Pretzels, Rose Hot Dogs, and Rose Soda; Wilda ran a booth that sold edible rose petals crystallized with sugar, Rose Petal Cake, and a platter of Rose Burgers—very rare-looking meat sandwiched between pink buns.

Colin and I shared a batch of the sugared petals; they were sweet and sticky, with a slightly bitter taste at the same time. It seemed like half the town kept coming up to us with more questions about our expedition to find Noelle. Even Henry seemed to have forgiven me.

"Tell me, Fiona. I hear she was wearing some weird *Little House on the Prairie* getup. Did she look ridiculous?" Henry asked me. "Sounds so creepy."

I decided I'd keep my promise to Noelle. I shook my head and said my line: "I'm just glad she's safe."

He eyed me. "I guess, considering everything, if you want your old job back, you can have it. There are only a few days left of the season, but If you show up on time, maybe I'll hire you to assist me in the cafeteria at Venice High, if you're lucky."

"That's okay," I said. "I think I've got a new job."

"Where?" He furrowed his brow.

"With Gus Jenkins, at his detective agency."

"I guess, if that suits you. Oh, I think I saw one of those kerfishes you like at a booth over there—it's a huge potato-and-rose-oil dumpling. Delicious."

"I'll be sure to try one," I said.

I walked back over to Sam. She was explaining more about the Noelle story to Chester's wife. "Well, the weird thing is, Noelle didn't even know the McBrides and the Parsils were distantly related. Like third cousins twice removed or something like that. Johnny Parsons—or Parsil, or whatever you want to call him—his grandparents had a huge falling-out with the McBride side of the family, and after that they were never in touch."

"What happened to him?" Chester's wife asked Sam. "That poor, lost soul."

"Noelle's parents had him committed to an institution. Technically he was guilty of kidnapping, but since he didn't hurt Noelle in any way, they decided not to press charges. He's still a disturbed, crazy guy, though."

"Noelle was lucky," I said to Colin as we walked along the booths that lined the street.

Neither Sam nor I had ever voiced it, but I knew that

through this whole scenario, she must have been thinking of our mom as much as I was. Noelle had been scared out of her wits, but she'd survived. She was fine. Our mom hadn't been so lucky. Why had Noelle survived, but not our mother? And why was Noelle lucky enough to have two living, breathing parents of her own? I knew it wasn't such a great thing to think these thoughts, but I couldn't help it. Even after this time and distance and everything that had happened, there were so many aspects of my parents' deaths that I still hadn't recovered from. I wondered if I ever would.

Colin asked if I wanted to go up on the Ferris wheel. "Sure," I said. He bought two tickets.

The sun had started to set; in the distance Noelle and Lacey were up on the podium, giving their Rose Queen speeches. We couldn't hear from where we were, and that was fine. The sky was so clear and the corn-fields stretched on so far that I almost felt like I could see all the way to New York.

"I'm sorry about that night by the fire, how I brought up your friends and Cleveland and all that," Colin said. "I didn't mean to make you uncomfortable."

"Oh, that's okay. Sometimes it's just hard to talk about. I guess it's because of our parents and every-thing . . . In some ways it's just easier to start over, without all those memories. To start a new life," I said.

"You and Sam really amaze me, how you've done that," he said. The Ferris wheel paused; our car swung in the wind at the top. From down below we could see

Ethel and Chester waving at us. Their antennae bobbed as they waved.

"You and your sister—you're really strong," he said. "I hope you guys know that."

"Sam is," I said. "But I don't think I'd say that about myself." Didn't he remember how many times I'd cried in the weeks since we'd moved to Venice? How I'd collapsed in his arms, sobbing like a little kid?

"I mean you, too," he said. "You're really strong."

No one had ever said that to me before. I couldn't even think of another compliment I'd rather hear. Maybe, despite everything that had happened, we would be okay. Maybe I wasn't just that crying, exhausted, grief-stricken girl who had packed up her father's car in Queens in her boxer shorts and shark slippers, wondering if she'd ever survive. We had survived; we'd made it here and started over.

"Where were you guys?" Sam asked us. She was drinking a bright red soda and eating a slice of Wilda's Rose Petal Cake. "We were looking for you."

"We rode the Ferris wheel," I said. "You can see all the way to Venice, Italy, from up there."

"Hey, check that out," Sam said, pointing in the direction of the podium. The mayor was just stepping down after finishing her speech, heading right for her husband, who waited a couple of feet away. He greeted her with a big hug. I gazed around the crowd and saw Callowe standing by himself, looking sulky.

"He broke it off," Gus explained through a mouthful of food.

Sam yawned. "This Rose Festival is making me sleepy."

"You girls better get some good rest tonight," Gus said. "You got a big day tomorrow at the Jenkins Agency."

"So I'm officially hired as your new secretary?" I asked.

Sam smirked at Gus. "We're both officially hired. Fern doesn't mind, since there's only a week left of the Rose Club season anyway. Gus and I worked everything out while you and Colin were off gallivanting around."

I gave Sam a quick, questioning glance that I hoped Gus wouldn't pick up on. Was she at all worried that spending more time around him could be dangerous for us? We still didn't know for sure what, exactly, he knew about us. Sam caught my glance and gave a quick, reassuring shake of her head that no, she wasn't concerned. Or maybe she thought we'd actually be *safer* sticking close to the one person who might be onto us.

"So you'll have two secretaries?" I asked Gus.

"Partners," Sam said.

"Assistants," Gus said.

"Assistants is all right," Sam said. "But down the road, you're going to be working for us."

When the speeches were all over and the bands had finished playing, we said good night to Gus, and Colin walked Sam and me home.

"Your first Rose Parade," Colin said. "What did you think?"

"It was pretty fun," I said. "In some ways this town is a lot more exciting than living in the city, I think."

He laughed, but I was telling the truth.

We arrived at our door. "Want to come in?" I asked him. "A game of Lorna Scrabble?" Colin had lost the last one we'd played by putting down *sesamoid*, which had turned out to be an actual word.

"All right," he said.

We stayed up till late that night playing the game— and laughing and talking and nursing our bellies, which were overstuffed with pink food and sugared petals.

"*Quergd*," Sam said, arranging her letters. "A squirrel who subsists only on Italian specialties, such as fettuccine, lasagna, and baked ziti."

Colin went next. "*Bezfos*. A Middle English term for two sisters who somehow manage, despite all the odds, to worm their way into the heart of a crazy, stodgy old town."

Then it was my turn. I stared around our living room, at the colorful antique furniture, my new tube top in a pile of folded laundry on the sofa, and my stuffed polar bear, Ed, one of the last things I'd grabbed from our house in Queens, resting on top of a bookcase.

"*Snervy*," I said. "An ancient word for a new home."